GUILTY REFLECTIONS II
WAR OF THE SOUL

TERREL CARTER

iDream Publications

Published by: iDream Publications
P.O. Box 28910
Philadelphia, PA 19151
ISBN 978-0-9835965-0-9
Copyright: 2010
Guilty Reflections II
Author: Terrel Carter
Editing and text formation by Sarah Caroline Morris
Cover designed by Tyrone Mitchell (aka Boohonik)
Cover Graphics by LJ of Strickly Graphics

PRINTED IN THE UNITED STATES OF AMERICA

ISBN: 0983596506
ISBN-13: 9780983596509

CreateSpace, North Charleston, SC

Dedication

I dedicate this book to:

My stepfather, John Skief, a man in my life who planted seeds of consciousness in me. Although at the time it seemed as if I didn't listen, I did, I just didn't understand. But now those seeds have taken root and grown, allowing me to become the man I am today, something that I will be forever grateful for. May God bless and protect your soul…

Acknowledgements

First of all, I'd like to thank the usual suspects for their love and support, my mother, Tonya, who's been my rock and a continuous source of love and support. To my father, Jamil, may Allah bless his soul. To my little girl, Shanté. Although she's a woman now she'll always be my little girl. And I can't forget the little jewel of my life, my beautiful granddaughter, Zya. I'd like to thank my sisters, Kimmy, Kalima, Liza, Nafisa, Najibah, and Lachelle. To my brothers: Kurt, Masai, Muhammad, Damani (rest in peace), Darien, and Ali. I'd like to give a shout to my family out in Newark, NJ: Qua, Kiesha, Nikki, Craig, and my Aunt Sis. Oh yeah, I definitely can't forget Ma Raine, thanks for holding the family down in D.C. and for your love and support. A special shout to all my nieces and nephews, Amir, Imani, Isaiah, Elijah, Elias, Naeem, Ashanti, Jamilah, Amir, Aziz, the twins, Ayanna, and little Damani.

There are a number of friends who've been riding with me over the years on the inside of these walls as well as the outside who I'd like to thank: My Homie Vern, Markese, Courtney Boyd (aka Juan), Shadeed (aka Tommy Lloyd). To my fellow writers, Yah Yah, thanks for the title, Jamo, and Lil Charlie, thanks for listening and I can't forget Bub, keep writing y'all!

I'd like to say what's up and thank my Homies from downtown 28th & the road, Brick, Charlie Block, and Gotti (aka Fat Tommy). To my Old Head Kareem (aka Pitbull Ha Ha Ha), Hasan, Wavy, and Ghani-thank you all for the love. To my Homies that's still with me on the outside, Mane, Tashi, Speed, Rich, Dave, Bap, O'Castro, my main man Jody, Cook, Dry, Manchild, Rip, Whitey, Hakim (aka Harry Hawkins), and my young buck G-Rap (aka Lil Gary).

My heartfelt thanks to Sarah for her time and patience in editing this piece. Nette for taking the pictures of the strip. And last, but not at all least, a big thank you to my best friend, the love of my life, my wife, Stacey. Words aren't sufficient to express my appreciation and gratitude. Thank you baby for being and meaning so much for and to me...

CHAPTER ONE

" All rise for the Honorable Judge O'Keefe," said the bailiff in the crowded courtroom.

A hush fell over the low murmur of voices as the crowd stood up and waited for the judge to enter. With his aged-lined face creased in a perpetual frown, Judge O'Keefe strolled god-like into the courtroom. The judge paused before taking a seat high up on his throne-like bench. His face was blank as his cold blue eyes scanned the brown faces that populated his courtroom. A cacophony of whispers replaced the brief silence as people picked up their isolated conversations once they were re-seated.

Rafique Johnson waited nervously at the defense table. His heart hammered loudly in his chest as he stared at the man who held his life in his hands. Whether he went home to his family or went back to jail to spend the remainder of his life there would be decided today, and his emotions were in turmoil. He tried in vain to relax, but it was difficult to do so, for within his mind optimism waged a silent war to the death with pessimism. On the optimistic side of the battlefront, his alibi witness, Buff, did an excellent job and as a direct result of that he felt good about his chances.

On the other side of this intense internal conflict, pessimism fought hard to gain ground. His life rested in the hands of a man who sat in judgment but knew him not, and only saw him not as a human being, but as a fact in one of the hundreds of cases he resided over. Add on the extreme racism that infects the entire criminal judicial system and you'd have a recipe for pessimism to win out, but this internal conflict would be long and hard with both sides gaining and losing ground.

Like a hungry vulture staring at a pride of lions devouring a fresh kill, Judge O'Keefe peered over the top of his horn rimmed glasses, cleared his throat, and banged down hard with his gavel. "Order in the court!" he shouted, bringing the courtroom to a nervous silence. He cleared his throat once more, his tired blue eyes zeroing in on Rafique.

"Mr. Johnson, would you please stand." Slowly rising to his feet, Rafique's throat became dry, and his palms began to sweat. With each passing second his anxiety levels increased, forcing his heart to beat harder and arousing a swarm of butterflies that took flight in the pit of his gut.

His voice robotic and devoid of emotion, Judge O'Keefe began to speak, "On the matter of the Commonwealth of Pennsylvania vs. Rafique Johnson, the petitioner's petition for a new trial has been denied."

Instantaneously the courtroom erupted with shouts of outrage and cries of dismay as Rafique's family and friends voiced their anger over the judge's decision.

In a futile attempt to speak over the shouts, the judge continued, "You have thirty days from this date to…Order in the court!" he shouted banging his gavel as he tried to quiet the crowd down. "You have thirty days from this date to file an appeal. This court proceeding is adjourned." The Judge slammed his gavel once more, got up from his seat and, without a backward glance, left the courtroom with his black robe billowing in his wake.

Rafique was devastated. It was as if he had been found guilty and sentenced to life all over gain. Not wanting to experience the piercing hurt of having to see and hear the anguish and heartbreak on the faces and in the cries of his loved ones, he turned to the sheriff and softly said, "Yo man, please get me the fuck out of here."

The sheriff placed the cuffs on Rafique's wrists and led him, head bowed, through a river of misery and out of the courtroom.

✲ ✲ ✲

Fourteen days had elapsed since that ominous day at court and Rafique was still agonizing over the outcome. Like a colony of termites infesting a wood shed, depression festered within his spirit, driving all hope away. He was on the verge of giving up. No one could bring him out of this state, not his uncle Joe-Joe or the handful of people he considered his friends. As the days dragged on, he withdrew more and more. He wouldn't go out on visits, he wouldn't answer his letters, and he wouldn't call home. His family and friends were worried sick as he stayed in his cell wallowing in self-pity, frustration, and pent-up rage. *Why me?* He thought, *why I got to spend the rest of my life in jail for some shit I ain't even do. This shit ain't right.* The answer to this question remained elusive and the negative emotions continued to intensify. The pressure of these trapped feelings boiled just beneath the surface. The strain of keeping them in check slowly whittled away with the weight continuing to mount, slowly it built until one day, two weeks after his court date, he could not hold back the rage and frustration any longer. Standing in front of his cell, his dark brown eyes smoldering with aggression, he stared at a young man walking towards him.

"Yo man, how come every time you walk by you peeping in my motherfucking cell?"

With a look of total surprise on his face, the young man replied, "What?"

"You heard what the fuck I said!"

"Yo, you trippin, you better get the fuck out of here."

"I'm trippin, huh?" Rafique asked as he inched aggressively closer.

The young man could see the situation spinning out of control. "Yo, man, I don't want no trouble."

"It's too late for that shit." Rafique left those words hanging in the air and, without warning, threw a wild overhand right catching the young man over the top of his left eye. Stunned with a slight cut running through his eyebrow, the young man stumbled backward. Quickly regaining his balance and his senses, he reached in his waistline, pulled out a six-inch, homemade ice pick and met Rafique head on.

Fascinated prisoners watched with a morbid curiosity as Rafique, blinded by rage and a sense of hopelessness, prepared to take out his frustrations on a young man who was in the same position as he was - powerless to confront the criminal justice system that he felt was holding him hostage. Rafique struck, releasing the pressure that had been building for days. His face cloaked with murderous intention, he swung wildly at the young man's head.

Baffled by the turn of events, the young man didn't let his anger and surprise at being attacked cloud his ability to defend himself. After Rafique swung another one of his wild over hand rights, the young man ducked and came back up to systematically drive the point of his ice pick again and again through brown clothing and flesh.

Blood seeped from Rafique's wounds, but he was unaware of it. His rage was so blinding and intense that he never saw the ice pick as the other man continued to poke holes through him. The adrenaline that coursed through his body blocked out all pain and he absorbed the punctures as if they were regular punches. Thinking it was sweat, Rafique ignored the blood that began to soak through his shirt and run down his body. The loss of this precious fluid began to take its toll as his swings became less frequent and more debilitating. Finally, too weak to even hold his hand up, he collapsed.

The young man, seeing that his attacker was no longer a threat, faded away into the crowd of onlookers. He paused briefly, passing off the bloody ice pick to one of his homies, before continuing to his cell where he walked inside and closed the door behind him. He paced back and forth in his small cramped up cell, pausing for a moment to light up a Newport. His mind raced as he flopped down on his flat, hard mattress and blew smoke rings towards the ceiling. *Damn, I hope that nigga ain't dead. I'm supposed to go home next year. If he dies, I know I ain't gonna get away with that shit. All them niggas that was out there, I know somebody gonna tell. Damn, out of all the niggas in this joint, why the fuck he come at me like that. Fuck that, I ain't tryin to go out like my Uncle Moose and let a nigga kill me in jail. Better that nigga dead than me. I did what I had to do.* Turning his radio on, he continued to fret. Like most young men who react instead of thinking things through, he thought about all the things that could go wrong, now that the deed was done. He closed his eyes and tried to erase those thoughts and go to sleep, but on this day, sleep would be hard to come by as thoughts of negative consequences plagued him.

✭ ✭ ✭

C/O Monique Thompson picked through a Styrofoam tray of half-consumed beef stew. Although she hadn't eaten all day, she had no appetite. She sighed as she slid her seat away from the lunch table, got up, and threw the picked over tray in the trash can. With her half hour lunch break over, she put on her DOC baseball cap low over her slanted eyes and pulled her ponytail through the back. Her black uniform pants clung tightly to her perfectly shaped round ass, drawing all eyes to her backside as she strutted out of the lunch room and down the Graterford hallway.

On most days she would revel in the attention from the male guards and prisoners alike, but on this day she ignored the lustful stares. The last fourteen days had passed by in blur as she tried to come to grips with one of the most disappointing days in her life. After sitting in courtroom 625 and hearing the judge utter one word – "denied"- all of the plans that she made with Rafique were for naught. *It ain't fair*, she thought. *How can this old white, wrinkled, dick-faced motherfucker sit in judgment of someone who comes from a world totally different from his? Who the fuck is he to say what the truth is and what ain't the truth? It ain't right.* Not only was she questioning the fairness of the judicial system, but she was also worried. Since the day of the hearing, when Rafique was led out of that courtroom, head bowed, in cuffs, she hadn't seen him at all. There had never been so much time that passed by without her seeing him. As one day followed the next, her concern grew. She checked to see if he was in the hole, but he wasn't there. She called his mother only to find out that no one in his family had heard from him either and they were just as worried as she was. Discovering this made her determined to check up on him. *I'ma cut through B-Block. This ain't like Rafique. He would've at least called home.* As these thoughts flashed through her mind, static followed by a metallic voice came to life over her walkie talkie. "Inmates fighting on B-Block. All available officers please respond."

That's just what I needed, an excuse to go on B-Block. Picking up her pace to a fast trot, Monique followed a group of guards who were converging on B-Block.

To Monique, the scene that unfolded in front of her eyes happened as if it were in slow motion. With the block locked down, her view was unobstructed as she gazed down the block. *Oh my God, they're in front of Rafique's cell.* Her heart thundered in her chest as she slowed down and began to walk. She paused for a moment, horrified, and watched as a fellow officer, his face beet red with exertion, ran towards her yelling, "We need a stretcher quick!"

She picked her pace back up and reached the circle of guards who surrounded a man lying stretched out on the floor in a puddle of blood. She looked down and covered her mouth as her breath got caught in her lungs. Becoming faint, she leaned on one of her co-workers for support. As waves of dizziness washed over her, what she saw cut her deep with pain. Her baby was lying stretched out on the floor, eyes closed with a peaceful look of death. It took everything in her not to lose her composure, as she fought off the urge to scream.

It seemed to take hours for the jailhouse medical team to finally arrive. Monique watched in shocked silence as the nurses strapped Rafique onto a gurney. After they had him secured, she moved into action by holding one of the handles. Making sure she took a position next to his head, she leaned down and whispered in his ear, "Rafique, you better not die on me. Baby, please hold on."

Minutes later, standing on the rooftop of the prison, she watched as a helicopter flew him off to a hospital. All of a sudden, as the pain became too much to bear and she could no longer contain herself, a tear traveled down the length of her ebony cheek.

✫ ✫ ✫

Oh shit! This motherfucker stabbing me, Rafique thought right before he collapsed.

"We need a stretcher!" As if he could hear someone shouting from far away, Rafique heard the C/O holler out for a stretcher. Slipping in and out of consciousness, he felt peaceful; all he wanted to do was sleep. The shouts became quieter and quieter, slowly fading into nothingness as he lost consciousness.

"Rafique, you better not die on me. Baby, please hold on." *Was that Monique?* He thought as he briefly regained consciousness. Never figuring out if it was or wasn't, he faded back out again.

The whirling of the helicopter blades was the next thing he heard as he opened his eyes. "He's regained consciousness!" one of the paramedics called out. "Rafique, can you hear me?" The paramedic asked him while grabbing hold of his hand. "Yeah," Rafique responded weakly. "Alright, hold on buddy, we gonna get you the help you need in a second."

Rafique nodded his head slowly before everything went black again.

CHAPTER TWO

Rafique awoke from a deep sleep and the first thing he noticed were the voices. Faint at first, they became clearer and clearer the more his consciousness returned. Sluggishly his eyes fluttered open and slowly came into focus. *Where the fuck am I?* He thought at seeing the familiar faces surrounding his bedside.

"Oh my God, Rafique! Ms. Tonya, he's up!" Tracey shouted as she squeezed his hand.

"How you feeling, baby? His mother asked as she stared into her son's eyes.

Dehydrated, he tried to swallow spit to lubricate his dry throat. Unsuccessful, his voice cracked as he spoke, "Some water please?"

"Some water? Hold up, baby. Shante, hand me that water bottle please and come over here and say hi to your father," his mother said.

Shante moved slowly, her shyness evident as she handed her grandmother a bottle of water. "Hi, Dad," she spoke, her eyes glued to the floor.

Rafique sat up in the bed and stared wide-eyed at his daughter. His hand trembled slightly as he accepted the water from his mother. Confusion and shock rattled him to his core. His eyes blinked rapidly in disbelief. Were his eyes playing tricks on him? *How is my daughter a little girl again? What the fuck is going on?* He thought as he took a hefty swallow of water. It felt cool and refreshing as it traveled down his parched throat, immediately bringing relief, a brief distraction, and allowing him to speak clearly.

Softly he spoke back to his daughter, "Hey, baby girl, what's up?" His voice masked the bewilderment well. He handed the water back to his mother and noticed for the first time the IV tubes extending from his forearms to the machines that surrounded his bed. *Where are the fucking guards?*, he thought as he shifted his gaze back to his daughter. Completely disconcerted, slowly he tore his eyes away from her and faced his mother.

"Where the guards at, Mom?"

"Guards? Rafique, you're at the hospital. Why would there be guards here?"

He ignored his mother's question and looked at Tracey before gazing again at his daughter. "Tracey, what you doin here? And how did Shante get so young?"

"Rafique are you okay?" Tracey asked, her thick eyebrows knotted together in a mask of concern.

"Tracey, remember what the doctor said about him being a little confused because of the coma," Rafique's mother interjected.

"Coma? What coma? I got stabbed in jail. I wasn't in a coma!"

"Jail? Rafique, baby, you weren't in jail. You were in a car accident. You've been in a coma for the past eight days," Tracey said.

"Huh? I've been in a coma for the past eight days? Car accident? Hold up...this ain't making no sense. I was in jail. I had a life sentence. Mom, where's Aisha and my son at?" His heart thundered in his chest like a bass drum in a marching band as butterflies the size of pigeons took to the air in the pit of his gut. His befuddlement mounted.

"Calm down, Rafique, you must have had a bad dream," his mother said as she gently stroked his forehead.

"Mom, it couldn't have been a dream. It was too real. I had a life sentence, I had a son, my father died, he had cancer. It wasn't a dream, it was real."

"Rafique that's all it was a dream. Your father is still alive in D.C. You haven't been to jail, and you don't have a son," Tracey said.

"Yo, man, why the fuck is you here anyway? Where's that nigga you live with?" he asked Tracey with venom dripping from his voice.

"Rafique, what are you talking about?" Tracey asked, her voice beginning to shake.

"Wait a minute..." his mother interrupted. "Rafique, you and Tracey live together. She doesn't live with anyone else. Look, baby, I think you should get some more rest. You've suffered a serious head injury. Let me go talk to the doctor and let him know you're up. Go ahead and get some more rest." Bending over, she kissed him lightly on the forehead. Before she left the room, Tracey followed his mother's footsteps and tried to kiss Rafique, too, but he turned his head away.

"Bye, Dad," Shante called out from the doorway.

"Alright, Tay, I'll see you when y'all get back."

Tracey didn't say a word as tears began to flow steadily down her face. After Shante and his mother left the room, Tracey lingered in the doorway staring at Rafique completely confused and hurt at his reaction towards her. Finally, after a few minutes had transpired, she too turned and left the room, leaving a totally befuddled Rafique with his thoughts.

Damn, what the fuck is going on? Am I losing my mind? This can't be real. As these thoughts ran through his mind, he began to check his upper body for knife wounds, but there weren't any. *Yo, this shit is crazy; I ain't got no stab wounds on me. Damn, all that shit was a dream. I ain't got no life sentence! My pop is still alive! It was just a dream!* The realization of what that meant caused him to smile. The most traumatic experience of his life wasn't real, but he could still remember everything from that dream as if it were a part of his memory. *Damn, this is crazy. I get to live my life knowing shit that it takes some motherfuckers fifty years to learn. I got to get out of this hospital. I got a lot of shit I need to do. I gotta go see my father, I gotta go see Aisha. I definitely gotta spend more time with my daughter now that I know how important that is. I still can't believe it, I' m actually home.* Tears of happiness left trails of salt down his cheeks as he lay back and closed his eyes. He yawned, as all excitement from the day began to take its toll. Drained emotionally, it didn't take him long to fall fast asleep.

✲ ✲ ✲

Tonya walked up to the office door of the doctor who was responsible for her son's treatment and tapped lightly on the door. "Excuse me, Dr. Reynolds."

Dr. Reynolds looked up from a sheaf of papers and smiled, "Uh, yes, Mrs. Johnson, how can I help you?"

"My son has just awakened," she said as she entered his office.

"Well, that's good. You can never tell with coma patients."

"Doctor, he's delusional, though. He keeps saying all these wild things about being in jail for life and being stabbed. He thinks his father is dead, I mean doctor, he's saying all kinds of crazy stuff."

"Mrs. Johnson, your son has been in a coma for a little over a week. He's just confused by a vivid dream. We've all experienced dreams that seem like reality. He'll be perfectly fine. I'll go up to check on him as soon as I'm finished up here."

"Thank you, doctor; I was beginning to become a little concerned."

"No need to be concerned, Mrs. Johnson, what your son is experiencing is perfectly normal under the circumstances."

With the doctor putting her mind at ease, Rafique's mother visibly relaxed. "I'll be in the waiting area after you've seen him, and doctor, thank you again."

"No problem, Mrs. Johnson," Dr. Reynolds responded as he got up and shook her hand. She flashed a smile and left the doctor's office feeling a lot better.

CHAPTER THREE

Empty the trash cans, dust and vacuum the floors eight to fourteen. Every night, eight p.m. to two a.m., five days a week. This was Rafique's job. Classical music played softly in the background while he rode the elevator of a center city skyscraper to the eighth floor. For the past seventy-five days since being released from the hospital, he was employed by Jefferson Office Cleaning Company, the same job he had before his accident.

A slight headache throbbed incessantly in his temples, a mild consequence from the head trauma he suffered in the crash. DING…a bell chimed softly, slightly louder than the music as the elevator came to a stop and the doors slowly slid open. Rafique stepped out of the elevator with a bag of cleaning materials slung over his shoulder, pushing a vacuum. Slowly he exhaled, took a seat in the lobby and closed his eyes. Gently but firmly he massaged his temples in an effort to ease the annoying pain. After about five minutes, the pain stopped. With his eyes still closed he didn't move; he just sat there. He loved the solitude of his job. It was the only perk of the $5.50 an hour gig. He hated the low pay, but it was work and it was all he had at the time. Before the accident the low wages didn't bother him because the four pounds of weed that his young buck C.H. sold for him in dime bags on 52nd Street supplemented his meager wages nicely.

Things hadn't been the same since the crash, though. The word on the street after the car accident had him clinging to life, doubtful of surviving, and as a direct result of that, C.H. went on a pill-popping, syrup-drinking binge for three months, effectively ruining Rafique's supplemental income.

Reflexively rubbing his temples again, he got up and plugged in the vacuum. The loud hum of the Hoover coming to life upset the silence of the empty floor as he ran it over the short haired, blue carpet of the lobby floor. Softly humming Al B. Sure's "Night and Day," he thought about his present situation. He was dead broke with no prospects of getting any money any time soon. Basically, his woman Tracey was taking care of him. She paid most of the bills. For the most part, he just chipped in whenever he got his measly check. Even after he woke up from the coma and treated her like trash in the hospital, she shook it off and continued to be there for him. Every time he opened his eyes, it was her dark browns that stared back at him, and now she was still playing her part by taking care of his broke ass. He felt like shit being broke and having to rely on his woman. So every morning he got up and pounded the pavement trying, without any luck, to find another job.

Damn, she's a real good girl, he thought as he unplugged the vacuum and began emptying all the waste paper baskets placed throughout the hallway and offices. *I can't believe I treated her like that about a fucking dream.*

The dream, the one that seemed so real, so vivid, to this day remained clear in his mind like another set of memories. It was as if one day his life split in two with one sprinting through ten years, creating memories as the other life lay dormant. Then suddenly, he was thrust back to his dormant life under completely different circumstances with these newly formed memories and being able to live those ten years again. It was almost enough to drive him crazy, but he kept repeating to himself that it was just a dream and that was enough to keep him sane.

The first several days after he woke up from the coma, his dream was all he could talk about, and whenever he would discuss it, he talked about it as it had actually happened. But after a while, the indulgent smiles started to take on looks of concern and he stopped talking about it, but the memories of that dream still plagued his every waking moment. This was why he hadn't attempted to hustle. Graterford's prison walls and life without parole still seemed too real to him.

The only person he could still feel comfortable talking to about his dream was his father. His father couldn't believe the changes that had taken place within his son. Rafique was talking to him, something he had been trying to get his son to do for years. So if it was a dream that got Rafique to do what he had been so unsuccessful at, then Jamil would listen to his son talk about his dream for the rest of his life if that's what he wanted to talk about.

Rafique emptied the waste paper baskets and smiled as his mind wandered back to the hospital and the day his father called. He could still hear the happiness in his father's voice when he answered the hospital room phone.

✰ ✰ ✰

"Hello."

"As salaam alaikum, Rafique?"

"Abbee, walaikum salaam, what's up man?"

17

"How are you?"

"I'm doing okay, I feel a lot better. I just be getting these migraine headaches. Other than that, I'm cool."

"That's good, I'm glad to hear you're doing okay. You had us worried out here when we got word that you was in a coma."

"I'm cool now, what's up with everybody, how's my brothers and sisters?"

"Everybody is doing okay. Lorraine was worrying me to death about you. They all keep asking about you, though. Liza and Kurt call everyday asking about you, too. I'll be sure to let them and Bobby know that you're doing okay and that it's cool to call."

Rafique sat up in the bed and considered whether or not to tell his father about his dream. *He gonna think I'm trippin just like everybody else. Come on man talk to your father. Use this as an opportunity to open up. You saw from the dream how close ya'll can become. Or do you want to wait til it's too late like you did in that dream?*

His heart began to hammer in his chest immediately as the thought of his father dying ran through his mind. Like an old memory called up from the deep recesses of his brain, the pain and the feeling of wasted time ripped through his body. *Calm down, it was only a dream. My father is alive on the phone with me right now.* The flash of this pain was enough though to convince him to open up and tell his father everything. As his heart rate began to subside, Rafique gripped the phone tightly and began to speak, "Ay, Abbee, I had this crazy dream while I was in that coma. I mean it was so real, I still be having trouble believing that it was a dream. I still be waking up thinking I'm in jail."

"In jail?"

"Yeah, that's what the dream was about. I dreamt that I had a life sentence for some shit I ain't even do. Abbee, it was so real! It got me looking at things in a whole new way."

"All this from a dream, huh?"

"Yeah, I mean even talking to you is easy for me now. You know how hard it was for me to open up to you. But that dream was like I lived a whole other life. I saw our relationship evolve. I lived through not being able to open up, to being able to share everything with you."

"Damn, this must have been a hellavu dream. I'm sitting here fucked-up listening to you. You sound like a completely different person."

"Abbee, it was like I had a chance to live my life, and then go back in time ten years. I mean it's like I've been given a second chance with ten years worth of experiences."

Jamil was silent for a moment as he processed what his son was saying. For twenty-three years he had been trying to bridge a seemingly impossible gap between himself and his middle son. Now, through a dream, it seemed as if the gap had evaporated. An overwhelming sense of relief and joy flooded his being as he began to speak, "Rafique, you just don't know how much it means to me to hear you express yourself to me. I've been regretting all your life the time that I didn't spend with you and how it has affected our relationship. I've been trying so hard to make things up to you so that we can bridge that gap created by my neglect. Hearing you right now is like a dream come true to me. I've been waiting a lot of years for this day."

Not knowing how to respond, Rafique changed the subject. "Abbee, I need for you to do me a favor."

"What's that?"

"I need for you to get your liver checked out."

"My liver? For what?"

"In my dream you died. You had a tumor the size of a golf ball on your liver. It killed you two months after you found out about it."

"Rafique, it was only a dream. You can't go through life as if things from a dream will actually happen. You can take things and learn from them, but only in the context of what it is, a dream."

"Yeah, you're right. I told you, though, that's how it has me. I mean, it was so vivid, it's like a memory."

"Well, keep in mind that it's only a dream. So when do you think you gonna be able to make it out here?"

"As soon as I get out the hospital and get things situated at home, I'll be out there. Plus, it's about time y'all met Shante. I really been neglecting to spend time with my little girl. It's funny how things repeat themselves with parents and their children. That's another thing I learned from that dream. I was repeating the same mistakes with my daughter that you made with me. Anyway, I'll be bring her out there as soon as I get things straight here."

"Alright son, I got to go now. My phone bill is high enough as it is. So you know, hurry up and get well so you can get out here."

"Alright, Abbee, I'ma see you soon. I love you, man."

"I love you, too, son. As salaam Alaikum."

"Wa laikum Salaam."

✲ ✲ ✲

"Ay, Rafique! You want something from the store?" His coworker Steve who cleaned floors one through seven had just stepped off the elevator and snapped Rafique out of his daydream.

"Naw, man, I'm cool."

"You sure?"

"Yeah, yeah, I'm cool, thanks though."

"Alright, homes." Stepping back onto the elevator, Steve was gone just as fast as he appeared.

Finished with his duties on the eighth floor, Rafique packed up his cleaning supplies and headed for the elevator and the next floor. The work night was young and he still had five floors to cover before his shift ended.

CHAPTER FOUR

In the midst of a late August heat wave, the streets of Center City Philadelphia were virtually deserted as the thermostat hovered past the one hundred degree mark. Chicky and Pete's Sport Bar and Grill was filled to capacity on this hot summer day as legions of baseball fans crowded the air conditioned bar to cheer on the Philadelphia Phillies. Battling the Atlanta Braves for first place in the division, the Phillies were in the middle of a heated pennant race. A championship starved city, Philadelphia fans rooted hard for their home team and came out in droves, even in one hundred degree heat, to show their support.

Filled with alcohol and the fervor of late August baseball, the fans were so caught up in the game they failed to notice the three individuals who, like everyone else in the bar, were decked out in Phillies jerseys, but seem to be uninterested in the game. They didn't cheer when the Phillies made a play and the bar patrons erupted in cheers. They didn't groan or shout out curses when the Braves made a play. Their focus was elsewhere. Sean, Ari, and Fuzz didn't care one bit about the Phillies or baseball.

It was just that this pennant race provided them with the perfect opportunity to do what they did best- steal.

Observing the drunken fans, all three searched for the perfect victim.

"Yo, Sean. There's a chump right there," Fuzz said in Sean's ear.

"Where at?"

"Right over there, the bitch with the Lenny Dykstra Jersey on, sitting at the bar. See her with the Prada bag hanging off her shoulder?"

Sean peered over the bar and nodded his head in agreement. He noticed immediately the three-karat diamond engagement ring on her finger and the matching diamond stud earrings, he knew that she had some money.

"Ari, see that bitch over at the bar with the Lenny Dykstra Jersey on? Go sit next to her and order three beers," Sean said to his girl and partner in crime.

Ari knew how to play the game and moved into action. She quickly navigated her way through the crowded bar, took a seat next to their target and ordered the beers. "Can I have three Miller Lites please?" she asked, flashing her dazzling, dimpled smile.

Seconds later, Sean and Fuzz arrived at the bar and stood in the space between Ari and the woman in the Lenny Dykstra jersey.

"Here are our drinks, gentlemen," Ari said as she turned around and handed Sean and Fuzz their beers.

Sean took a sip, placed his bottle of beer back on the bar and waited for Fuzz to move into position. Taking a position right behind Sean, Fuzz gave up a perfect block in case somebody happened to look towards them.

"IT'S BACK, BACK, BACK, BACK...
HOMERUN LENNY DYKSTRA!

AND THE PHILLIES HAVE TAKEN
A THREE-TO-TWO LEAD
IN THE BOTTOM OF THE NINTH!"

The bar exploded into cheers as their team went up on the Braves. At that same instant Sean went to work. Expertly, he reached over to his right, grabbed the zipper of the woman's Prada and smoothly unzipped it. His fingers worked deftly, like those of a surgeon, feeling through her pocketbook in search of her purse. *Got it,* he thought as he delicately removed the purse. Even if she were sober, she wouldn't have felt a thing. So with her blood alcohol level way past the legal limit, she didn't have a chance. With the crowd remaining totally absorbed in the game, Sean, leaving the woman's money in place, removed her American Express card and smoothly zipped her Prada back up, after putting her purse back inside. Sean winked at Ari, then grabbed his bottle of beer and headed for the front door with Ari and Fuzz close behind him.

✡ ✡ ✡

With the heat and humidity at extreme highs, 52nd Street was unusually quiet and sparsely populated. A few brave souls endured the unpleasant weather as they moved slowly from shop to shop, picking up odds and ends. Street vendors- always on the hustle- braved the heat as well, with their big, brightly colored beach umbrellas providing a little relief from the oppressive heat.

"Hey, Rafique!" Lisa called out, one of the brave souls who traversed up and down the strip in the blazing afternoon sun.

Rafique turned in the direction of the familiar voice and smiled at the sight before him. "Damn, Lisa, what's up girl? Looking all good," he replied, his arms held wide open as he approached her.

She walked into his arms, pressed her soft body against Rafique's and squeezed him tight. "I heard about your accident," she said in his ear. "I'm glad to see you're doing better."

Reluctantly releasing his embrace, Rafique stepped back and looked at her. Her skin the color of burnt copper glistened with sweat. Deep dimples marked her cheeks as she smiled warmly. His eyes traveled from her short cut curly hair to her bright red colored toenails, drinking in all the delicate distinctions of her body. "So, what's up? What you doin' out in all this heat?" he asked.

"I just came out to buy my nephew a pair of Jordan's. What you doin' out here?"

"To be truthful, I can't even remember. After running into you, ain't shit else registering."

She blushed before she spoke. "Rafique, go head with that. Ain't you still with that girl?"

"Yeah, but what that got to do with me and you? Don't you got a man?"

"Yeah, but I'm ready to kick his nut ass to the curb."

"Well, me and sis is doing alright, but like I said what me and you do ain't got nothing to with me and her."

"Boy, you crazy."

"Maaannn, I'd be crazy if I didn't try to holla at your fine ass. Look, Lisa, I ain't looking for no love connection, but I do dig you. So let's just take this one step at a time. You never know what the future might hold. Plus, I ain't asking you to put the brakes on your life. You can do what you want, just keep the side door open for your boy. Is you number still the same?"

"Yeah."

"Well, as soon as I get a chance, I'm gonna call you and we can talk about this some more."

"Alright, make sure you call me, too."

"Oh, I will."

"Alright then," Lisa said as she turned to walk away.

"Damn, I can't get a hug before you leave?"

She stopped in her tracks, turned back around and again walked into his arms. He embraced her tightly and ran his fingers up and down the soft fabric of her tennis skirt before letting them come to rest on her ample backside. He kissed her lightly on the neck, tasting salt as the smell of Liz Claiborne perfume drifted lazily up his nostrils. "Alright, Lisa, I'ma call you," he said as he released her and watched her walk seductively away. *Damn, she nice,* he thought as he tore his eyes away and began walking in the opposite direction.

✲ ✲ ✲

♬ HERE WE GO YO,
HERE WE GO YO,
SO WHAT'S SO WHAT'S THE
SCENARIO ♬

As The Tribe Called Quest and the Leaders of The New School's smash hit, "The Scenario," pumped loudly from the factory stereo system in his 1990 Honda Accord, Sean cruised slowly down 52nd Street. They had just left Byron's, where they were getting IDs made. Byron had an illegal ID shop in his mother's basement where he hooked up any kind of ID you needed. On this day, they needed an ID for Ari to match the credit card they had just stolen. All three were in a good mood. They were on their way to the mall to bust the credit card.

Fuzz sat in the back seat nodding his head to the loud music, staring absently out of the back window. *Is that Lisa,* he thought, *it damn sure is. Who the fuck is that nigga she hugging?* Angrily he stared out the window, watching as some dude rubbed up and down his girl's body. *That's Sean's nut ass homie Rafique,* he thought as Rafique turned and began walking away. At the same time Sean spotted his man and made a u-turn. Pulling up beside him, he slowed down and Ari rolled the passenger side window down. "Rafique!" she called out as Sean came to a stop.

Rafique heard his name, turned and saw his friends. He smiled and walked towards the car. Double parked now, Sean and Ari got out the car. "Hey Rafique," Ari said as she gave him a hug. "How are you?" She looked into his eyes with a sincere look of concern.

"I'm cool, I see you still lookin good as ever," Rafique responded, causing Ari to smile.

"What's up, homie," Sean said, gripping Rafique in a bear hug.

"What's up, man," Rafique responded.

"You had a nigga scared to death, that's what. You look good, though, you cool?"

It was at that moment Rafique noticed who was sitting in the back seat. *What the fuck he got this nigga with him for? This nigga is a fucking rat. Here I go again with this dream shit.*

Rafique shook the thoughts off. "Yeah, man, I'm fully recovered. I'm just trying to put things back on track. I still got that punk ass job that ain't paying shit. You know C.H. fucked my weed pack up. The nigga thought I was dead. So you know Tracey's been holding me down since I got out the hospital."

"Yo, man, I want to apologize for not coming to see you at the hospital."

"Don't worry about it."

"Naw, let me make it up to you. Take a ride with us."

"Take a ride? I don't know about all that. I told Trace I'd be right back after I paid the phone bill."

"Come on, man, we just got some work and we're headin out to the mall. We can pick up Tracey something real nice. She'd be cool after that. Plus you can call her and just let her know you with us when we get out of the mall."

As Sean was saying these things, Fuzz testifying against him flashed through his mind. *I can't live my life letting shit from a dream dictate what I do.* "Alright, man, I'm going."

"That's what's up. Ari, let Fique sit up front with me."

"You lucky I like you, Rafique," Ari said, smiling as she opened the back door.

Rafique got in the front and looked to the back seat. "What's up, Fuzz?"

"What's up, Fique," Fuzz said, camouflaging his hate. "How long you been out the hospital?"

"A little over two months."

This bitch ass nigga, putting his hands all over my girl, Fuzz thought with a fake smile plastered across his face. "Damn, man, I'm glad you pulled through."

"So what's up, Fique? You ready to get this money?" Sean asked as he started the car up and pulled off. With the radio on blast, Rafique just nodded his head, rolled the window back up, and leaned against the head rest as the AC cooled the inside of the car down. Closing his eyes, flashes of Fuzz on the witness stand pointing him out tormented his thoughts the whole ride to the mall.

CHAPTER FIVE

"Things are a lot better now since he got out the hospital," Tracey said while sitting in the kitchen talking to her girlfriend Buttons on the phone.

"Yeah, well he just ought to be. He treated you like shit when he woke up," Buttons replied.

"I know, but he was a little confused because of the coma. He got better, though, as the days went on. Buttons, you know what though, he still be acting a little distant."

"Did you say something to him about that?"

"No, hold up a minute," taking the phone from her ear and pressing it to her chest, Tracey hollered into the living room. "Tim-Tim sit your ass down and watch that damn TV before I come in there and whip your behind!" Tracey put the phone back to her ear and continued her conversation with Buttons. "Yeah girl, sorry about that, Tim-Tim running around like a damn park ape. But, no, I haven't mentioned it to him. Rafique is the kind of man that if something's bothering him, he'll tell me when he's ready. So, you know, I'll wait til then."

"Is he taking care of you in other areas?" Buttons asked, laughing lightly.

"Oh, definitely, he providing all the dick I can handle. It seems like he got hornier since he came home. We be doing it like three and four times a day."

"For real, girl? Shit, maybe I should hit Marshon upside the head and put his ass in a coma. Cause he definitely need to work this thing out some more. He got a bitch playing with toys."

Both girls broke out into a fit of laughter.

"Buttons, you crazy," Tracey said in between laughs. "Tim-Tim, didn't I tell you to sit your ass down?" Tracey yelled out to her son. "This boy gonna drive me crazy. He got too much energy." The phone beeping in her ear interrupted the conversation. "Buttons, hold on a minute while I answer the other line."

"Alright."

Tracey clicked over to her other line. "Hello."

"Tray, what's up? Look I paid the phone bill, but I'ma be a minute. I'm at the mall with Sean and Ari."

"Out the mall, what you doing out there?"

"Come on with all these fucking questions, I'ma see you in a little while, alright."

"Yeah, whatever."

"What? You got an attitude?"

"No."

"Alright, I'ma see you in an hour or two."

"Alright, Rafique."

"Alright, I love you."

"I love you too."

Tracey clicked back to Buttons, took a deep breath, and slowly exhaled. "Yeah, girl, that was Rafique calling me from some mall with his friend Sean and Sean's girl Ari."

"Sean, the light skin one I like, right?"

"Yeah."

"He probably out there with a girl on a double date."

"Buttons, I really don't need to hear that kind of shit."

"Oh, excuse me for being concerned."

"Anyway, where your man at?"

"In the front room watching that damn TV like he's always doing. I could walk past his tired ass naked and he wouldn't even flinch. Him and that damn baseball. That's alright, though- if he keep this shit up I'ma have to find me somebody else that know how to take care of a bitch."

"Girl, you ain't leaving Marshon. Why don't you just tell him how you feel?"

"I got to tell a grown ass man that he supposed to fuck his woman? Tracey, I'm tir—,"

"Tim-Tim! Look, girl, I'm sorry, let me call you back. This crazy little motherfucker jumping up and down on my leather couch.

"Alright, girl, call me back later on. I'm getting ready to go in there, turn off that baseball game and take me some dick."

"Buttons, you crazy. Bye, girl."

"Bye, Tracey."

Tracey hung up the phone, got up from the kitchen table and stormed into the living room. Five-year-old Tim-Tim saw his mother approaching and knew that he was in trouble. He immediately stopped jumping on the couch.

"Naw naw, it's too late now. I told you to sit your ass down!" Tracey shouted as she grabbed him by the arm. "Now you got to take your ass to bed."

"I don't want to go to bed, mommy," Tim-Tim said as the tears began to flow.

"Alright, well sit your ass down and watch these damn cartoons."

"Okay. I love you, mommy."

Tracey just smiled and shook her head. *He gonna be a mess when he gets older,* she thought as she sat down next to him on the couch. Getting the attention that he so desperately craved, Tim-Tim put his thumb in his mouth and snuggled close to his mother. Tracey sighed and hugged her son tight as they both became absorbed into the TV show.

☆ ☆ ☆

The quarter moon-shaped like the blade of a scythe-glowed ominously in the pitch blackness of space as Sean pulled up in front of Rafique's front door. Sean had already dropped Fuzz off and this was the last stop before he and Ari went home. He turned the radio down and looked at Rafique. "Yo, man, you cool?"

"Yeah, actually today was a good day."

Sean chuckled, "It damn sure was. Look man, this game we playing is sweet. You need to get down with us."

"I'm cool, man, plus I don't feel too comfortable around your man."

"Who Fuzz? If that's a problem, I ain't got no problem cutting that nigga off. Plus man, you already know how to pick pocket."

"Man, I ain't never did that shit before."

"Yes you did, we all did. Remember how we use to always be picking each other when we were younger. Shit you were the best out of all of us. It's the same thing."

"Shit if it is."

"Look, man, I'm telling you. Trust me, it's the same shit."

"Let me think about it. I'ma get back with you and let you know."

"Alright, man, I hope you decide to ride because we family. We might as well keep this paper in the family."

"Alright man, I'ma let you know. Look, I got to go. I was supposed to have been home. It's like eleven o'clock. Tracey gonna be bitching."

"Not after you give her what you got her."

"Yeah, you right about that. Alright, Ari, take care lil sis."

"Bye, Rafique," Ari responded.

Rafique got out the car as Sean popped the trunk. He walked to the back of the car, got his shopping bags and closed the trunk. Ari was just getting in the front seat as Rafique turned and walked towards his front door. He turned back around and waved as he approached the front steps. Sean beeped the horn and pulled off as Rafique headed up the stairs.

Rafique opened the front door to his apartment. He could see the front room light was on and he could hear the TV. *Tracey must of waited up for me,* he thought, as he stepped out of the small vestibule and smiled at the sight that lay before him. Stretched out on the couch sound asleep was Tracey. He left the bags at the entrance of the vestibule, and quietly crept towards her and pulled out the jewelry box he had in his jean pocket. Opening it up, he pulled out a diamond tennis bracelet and dropped the empty box to the floor. Although Tracey was a hard sleeper, he didn't want to take any chances of awakening her before he did what he was attempting to do. Upon reaching her, he stooped down and gently grabbed her wrist that dangled off the side of the couch. He calmly clasped the bracelet around her wrist next to her watch. He stood and softly shook her awake. "Tracey, get up."

Her eyes slowly fluttered open as she sat up with an attitude. "Rafique, you said you'd be home in an hour or two, and it's almost…" looking at her watch, her eyes lit up with surprise. "Oh, my god, baby, it's beautiful.

"You like it?"

"Do I like it? I love it. How did you get it?"

"Come on, man, that ain't important."

Getting up, Tracey gripped her man tight, "Baby, could you wait for me in the bedroom while I freshen up?" she said in his ear.

"You getting in the shower?"

"Yeah."

"How bout I join you?"

"That sounds like a good idea to me," as these words escaped her mouth, she happened to take a glance toward the vestibule. "Damn baby, what's in all them bags?"

"Oh, that's some clothes for me, you, Shante and Tim-Tim. There's some shit in there for me to sell, too. We can go through all that tomorrow. Go on now and get in that shower."

Releasing her embrace, she smiled and strutted sexily to the bathroom. Slowly shaking his head Rafique watched her walk away before he walked to the bedroom and got undressed.

Stepping into the steam filled bathroom, he shook his head thinking, *Tracey with this hot ass water.* Taking off his thick burgundy terry cloth robe he laid it across the toilet seat before opening the shower curtain.

Turning towards him, her face spoke sex as the steaming hot water rained down upon her back. Getting in the shower and closing the curtain behind him, he moved to the back of the tub turning to avoid the hot water. "Tracey, turn down the hot water some, this shit is too hot."

"Too hot? Rafique this water ain't hot," she laughingly responded while splashing him.

"Come on, man, stop playing," Rafique said jumping back, almost losing his balance. "See, you almost made me fall."

"Alright, alright, I'ma turn it down," she said, reaching for the hot water knob. "Is that better for you?"

"Yeah, this how the water suppose to be for normal people. Something wrong with your skin or something."

"Oh, something wrong with my skin, huh? You don't like how I feel?"

Rafique moved towards her, reached out and pulled her to him. "You know I ain't mean it like that. I love the way you feel." Passionately he placed a wet kiss on her forehead, then moving to her neck, kissing, sucking, and slowly licking.

"Uuummm," she moaned as his hands slid up and down her wet body.

They stood directly under the shower nozzle as the water rained upon them, cooling the rising heat of their bodies. As his mouth and tongue covered her with kisses, his hands explored every inch of her, gently rubbing, squeezing, and massaging. At the same time, she reached down with both hands and began to stroke his manhood. Fed up with the foreplay, Rafique wrapped his hands around her and gripped her ass. He picked her up, spun around and penned her to the wall. Wrapping her legs around his lower back, she reached down and guided him into her.

"Uuhhh, it feels so good, baby," she cooed in his ear as she flicked her tongue in and out of it.

"You like how this feels?" he gasped.

"Yes, ooooo, yes I like it, baby, don't stop," she said with her voice pleading.

With their bodies entwined in a lover's lock of pleasure, they lost themselves in each other, forming a union of love.

After a heavy dose of some serious lovemaking, the two laid in bed, totally spent. With her head resting comfortably on his chest, she slowly raked her fingernails across his abdomen and kissed him slowly on his chest.

"Don't start nothing you can't finish, Tray."

"I can't finish? From the look of things, you the one that's done."

"Yeah, say that shit in about an hour."

"An hour? Boy, shut up. Rafique can I ask you something?"

"Yeah, what's up?"

"Promise me you won't get mad."

"Get mad? Come on, man, I ain't gonna get mad. What's up?"

"Alright, remember after you woke up in the hospital and you was treating me all nasty?"

"Yeah, but I had just woke up from a coma. I was trippin."

"I know baby it ain't that, it's just that although you've been better since that day, you still been kind of, like, distant towards me."

Rafique was silent for a moment. He knew exactly what she was talking about. It was that dream that had him acting that way. Try as he might, he couldn't shake it. He couldn't shake the hurt and feelings of betrayal that lingered from when she crossed him in that dream. *Maybe if I just tell her about it, let it all out, I'll be able to get rid of all these fucked-up feelings.*

"Lift your head up, baby, so I can sit up." Tracey lifted her head and sat up with him. "Remember when I first woke up and I was talking all crazy about being in jail. Tracey that dream had me a little fucked up. And to be truthful, it still fucks with me. You see, man, in that dream you crossed the shit out of me. I mean, you was pregnant when I went on the run for a homicide. The fucked up part was when you let a nigga talk you into killing our child. Tracey, you moved in with this dude and I had only been gone like two months. And on top of that I was risking my freedom by coming back damn near every weekend just to see you and you still crossed me."

"Baby, it was just a dream, though, it wasn't real."

"I know. I know, it's just been kind of hard for me to shake those fucked-up feelings. Look, baby, I'm sorry if I've been acting distant towards you. You been like a rock for me and you don't deserve to be treated like that. From now on, I'm going to make a serious effort to treat you like you deserve to be treated."

"Don't get me wrong, you haven't been treating me bad, far from it. You've actually been treating me real good. It's just that things ain't been how they were before you got hurt. It's more like a feeling than anything. Baby, I just want to love you and I want you to love me, and I don't want anything to stand in between that love."

"It won't, trust me. Plus I feel like since I shared this with you things can start getting back to how they were. You feel that?"

"Feel what?"

Rafique rolled on his side and pressed up against her. "That."

"Boy, you crazy."

"I told you in about an hour. Talk that shit to me now." Tracey laughed as he began kissing her, starting a brand new round of lovemaking.

CHAPTER SIX

The grumbling of his stomach reminded Rafique that he hadn't eaten since the morning. Checking his watch, he turned off the vacuum and headed for the elevator. It was time for his lunch break.

Carrying a turkey hoagie, a bag of plain chips, and a sixteen-ounce bottle of Mountain Dew, he entered the cafeteria. He scanned the lunchroom and spotted one of his co-workers, Steve, and another man he didn't recognize sitting in the far corner. He slowly started walking that way. The closer he got, the more the stranger began to look familiar. Although he couldn't see his face, what he could see began to match a vague image of a man that had been trapped in his mind-from the rusty brown dreads to the melanin rich skin tone to the slightly pudgy frame of his body. Once he was in range and he heard the man's voice, his heart began to hammer in his chest causing the image in his mind to become crystal clear. *Oh shit, it's Kenyatta. What the fuck is going on?*

"Yo, Fique," Steve called out, interrupting his thoughts, "what's up, man?"

"What's up, Steve," Rafique responded as he walked up on the table.

"Yo, man, this is my uncle Kenyatta. He just came home from doing a twenty year bid. He just started today."

"What's up, youngblood?" Kenyatta said in a deep baritone voice. In a mild state of shock, Rafique continued to stare.

"Yo, Fique!" Steve called out snapping Rafique out of the fog of shock.

"Oh, damn, my fault. What's up, old head? Ay, look, I'll be right back. I got to go the bathroom," Rafique said as he set his food down on the table and made a hasty retreat.

Kenyatta watched Rafique hurry to the bathroom. He turned to his nephew and asked, "What's up with your boy, Steve? He's kind of strange."

"Naw, Uncle Yatt, he's cool. He was just in an accident, though. He was in a coma and everything. Ever since he got out the hospital he be zoning out from time to time."

Still watching Rafique, Kenyatta slowly nodded his head as his nephew's friend disappeared into the bathroom.

Slapping cold water on his face, Rafique stared at his reflection. *What the fuck is going on? That's Kenyatta from my dream. This shit is crazy. I think I might be losing my mind. Calm down, man, you reading too much into this.* As the cold water dripped from his chin, Kenyatta's face and words from his dream began playing in his mind like an old memory.

✵ ✵ ✵

"Ay, Kenyatta, my father sent me this quote from a poem that said 'Stone walls do not a prison make, nor iron bars a cage. Prison is in your mind.' I never really could understand that quote until now," Rafique said, taking a seat on the edge of Kenyatta's bed.

"I know about that quote. I got it in here somewhere written down. What do you think it means?"

"Well to me it means that your thinking can be trapped in a box. It means that you can be indoctrinated into looking at things one way and one way only."

Kenyatta smiled and nodded his head, "To me, that quote means that people have been socialized to the point where they place limitations on themselves, which hold them back from reaching their full potential. It's like their minds have locks on them that they don't have the keys to. So you have people walking around physically free but mentally locked up. You see all this concrete and steel keeping us behind these walls, that ain't prison. Prison is the restrictions that we place on ourselves that won't allow us the thinking that's required to regain our physical freedom." Kenyatta paused as he lit up a Newport and took a deep drag. Slowly exhaling the smoke, he began to speak again. "Ay, Rafique, you remember when you were in school? Bear with me for a minute. You know how I get when I get going jumping from one topic to the next. But can you remember when they taught you to believe that Abraham Lincoln was this benevolent man that freed the slaves because it was the morally right thing to do?" Rafique nodded his head in response.

"Well that was some bullshit. The truth is what he did was issue a proclamation saying that all slaves were free in the states that were no longer loyal to the union. So in all actuality, he freed no slaves because he had no power in those states. Those states that rebelled from the union were called the Confederacy. They had their own laws army, president and money. Lincoln freeing those slaves would be like me telling you that your kids can't watch TV after seven o'clock. I don't have any control over your household. So me saying that don't mean shit. You follow me?"

Rafique nodded his head as Kenyatta took one last drag from his cigarette before putting it out. Kenyatta blew the smoke out and continued.

"The reason why Lincoln even bothered to do that was to gain the support of the European Nations that had already abolished slavery, particularly England and France. The man was in the midst of a civil war and if the Europeans supported the Confederacy, it could've been a very good chance the Union would have lost the war. So really the Emancipation Proclamation was a frivolous political ploy. Here look at this." Kenyatta pulled out a sheet of paper with one of Lincoln's speeches printed on it. "Just read the part that's highlighted."

"My paramount objective is to preserve
the Union, not to save or destroy Slavery."
Abraham Lincoln

After reading the quote, Rafique looked up and handed it back to Kenyatta.

"You ever read the Thirteenth Amendment – the one that supposedly abolished slavery?" Kenyatta asked, taking the sheet of paper from Rafique's out stretched hand. Rafique shook his head.

"Here it is, read it." Kenyatta said handing Rafique another sheet of paper with the Thirteenth Amendment written on it.

THIRTEENTH AMENDMENT
Neither slavery nor involuntary servitude
Except as a punishment for a crime, where of the party
shall have been duly convicted shall exist within the
United States or any place subject to their jurisdiction.

"You see, youngblood, the key sentence in the amendment is: 'Except as a punishment for a crime where of the party shall have been duly convicted.' Young brother, slavery was never abolished. The federal government was intimately involved in establishing and perpetuating slavery. It passed laws like the Fugitive Slave Act and the Missouri Compromise of 1850. These laws helped further slavery and maintain a system that ultimately led to this country being the wealthiest on the earth. Think about it, youngblood, for hundreds of years this country had free labor which allow them to stack their coffers full of profit." Kenyatta stretched and looked at Rafique and continued, "Alright, youngblood the history lesson for today is over. It's time for me to take my beauty nap. Stop by later on so we can kick it some more."

"Alright, Yatt" Rafique said as he got up and headed for the cell door.

Rafique splashed some more water on his face as the image of Kenyatta faded from his mind.

His heart still hammered in his chest as he continued to stare at his reflection. *Maybe Steve told me about him before. That's why he was in my dream. How could I know what he looked like though? I never saw him before? Steve probably showed me a picture of him and I just forgot because of the accident. Yeah that's probably what happened.*

Rafique felt good about this explanation, he smiled at his reflection as his heart rate subsided. He took a deep breath, splashed his face one last time and headed back to the table.

☆ ☆ ☆

"Yo, Fique, you right on time. My uncle over here trippin'. He mad at the white man cause of all the time he did. Not that I blame him, I would be mad, too. But everything ain't the white man's fault. We can't keep blaming the white man for all our problems. We got to start taking responsibility for our actions."

"You see, nephew," Kenyatta began. "That's your problem. You believe the perception that's been projected to you. Problem is perception ain't always reality. You got to pull back the covers to see what's really going on. Look at it like this: poverty is one of the reasons why our communities are plagued by crime. Can you agree with that?"

"Yeah," Steve replied.

"Okay, now ask yourself what would happen if there were no crime. Now really take your time and think about that before you answer. I know all the obvious things are probably running through your mind, but try to think of the less obvious things that are just as important. Try to think of all the people who would be affected negatively by the sudden stoppage of criminal acts. Think of all the money that's generated and flows through this economy as a direct result of illegal gains. Now, imagine if that were to stop. With all this in mind, you'll begin to see that it's in a lot of people's best interest to maintain a criminal element."

"Okay, I can see all that, but people still know right from wrong. They just choose to do the wrong things," Steve said defiantly.

Rafique didn't say a word. He just looked on, enjoying the conversation and his hoagie.

"Do they really? What you just did was answer a complicated problem with a simplistic answer. So the question remains, how do you get people to go against what they know to be right? I'll tell you how. You sprinkle in a heavy dose of self-hatred and hopelessness, along with flooding the community with drugs and alcohol and enough guns to supply a small army. Mix all that with rampant materialism and you'll have a recipe for self-destructive behavior."

"Yeah, but Unc, look at me. I ain't never took no drugs, robbed nobody or went to jail, and I come out of those same places as the ones that do all that shit."

"My poorly informed nephew, everyone won't succumb to these traps. Only a certain percentage of the population will. Think about it, how would it look if every black man in the country went to jail? Look at it like this, say you're a fox-hunter laying fox traps in the forest. You're not going to catch every fox in the forest. You'll only catch a percentage of them.

You see nephew, there are many pitfalls and obstacles in the pathway of becoming a free thinking black man. I mean it's so many of them that if you don't fall into the trap of the pen, early grave, drug addiction or AIDS, you'll succumb to the trap like the one you've fallen into."

"What trap? I ain't fall into no trap."

"Yes you have. You've fallen into the most dangerous one of them all, the trap of ignorance. How much do you read nephew? I bet it ain't much, and when do you read, you read things that reinforce your ignorance."

"Unc, man, you always talking this Black Man, revolutionary shit. You been to jail, read some books and now you walking around this motherfucker like you Malcolm X. You a fucking janitor, fucked-up and broke just like me. Show me how to get some money without going to jail. Yeah, you right, I don't read that much, but we in the same position-the Black Man scholar and the broke ass janitor.

"Don't get upset, nephew, this ain't no personal attack on you. But you're right, we are in the same position. But there's a difference. You see, I've freed myself in every sense of the word. I've broken those mental chains that our people have been crippled by and as a direct result of that I can think freely. Do you know that there was this behavioral scientist called B.F. Skinner? This dude was the best in that field. He said: 'You can delude a people into thinking they have free will and still control them.' I'm not one of those people who's being controlled. So although I don't have all the superficial things in this life that defines success in this country, I'm cool with my station in life. You see, I define success by reaching the goals you set for yourself. My goals are to reach as many young brothers as I can so that I can show them how they've been socialized to the point where they place limitations on themselves that won't allow them to reach their full potential. In doing this I feel fulfilled. My life has meaning."

Oh shit, that's some of the same things he was saying to me in my dream, Rafique thought, his mouth hanging open as he listened to Kenyatta speak.

"Oh, so because you using these big ass words and you quoting some shit from one of them jail house books you was reading, you think you gonna change my mind?"

"Naw, nephew, all I can do is share with you what I've learned. It's up to you what you do with the information. Look man, I ain't trying to belittle you, I'm just trying to get you to see things for what they are."

"He's right, Steve," Rafique said finally joining the conversation after taking another bite of his hoagie.

"What? Naw, not you, you the same dude that be out there in the middle of all that dumb shit," Steve said to Rafique, his anger mounting.

"You know what, I can't deny that, and that's something that I've been fighting with myself about, especially since I got out the hospital. It seems like after I woke up out of that coma, I've been seeing things in a whole new way. It's like right now I got two souls battling for the possession of my being. I mean I'm like in the middle of an internal tug of war. It's like I'm being pulled in two different directions. On the one hand, I'm this street motherfucker that's into all that street shit, but on the other hand I got this consciousness in me that's in direct opposition to everything that I've been." Rafique was extremely careful not to mention his dream as being the source of this new found consciousness.

Silence followed for a moment as Steve and Kenyatta digested what Rafique had said. Rafique finished off his hoagie with a hefty swallow of soda. He watched them both and waited on a response.

"You know what youngblood, you're going through what a lot of people go through once they become conscious. I went through the same thing. It's very difficult to let go of something that you've been holding on to for the better part of your life. This is why it seems that there are two souls residing within you. This is why it seems that you're a walking contradiction. Fear not, young brother- the more you study, the more you'll learn, and the freer your thinking will become. Eventually, you'll reach the point where you'll be a man with one soul, who's not living a life of contradiction. If you keep striving for it, you'll reach it, trust me."

Rafique gathered up his trash, stood up and extended out his hand to Kenyatta. "Yo, man, I'm glad I got a chance to meet you. I really appreciated this conversation. It's given me a lot to think about."

"It's good to have met you, too," Kenyatta said as he firmly shook Rafique's hand. Rafique released his grip and turned to Steve. "Alright, Steve. Yo, man, your uncle is a hellavu dude. You can learn a lot from him."

"Yeah, whatever, man," Steve said shaking Rafique's hand. He was still upset about the conversation. Leaving Steve and Kenyatta behind, Rafique took his trash with him, dumped it in the garbage can and left out of the lunchroom. While he headed back to the elevator, his mind replayed everything that had just transpired. A chill ran up and down his spine as a strange sense of déjà vu flooded his being. Rafique suppressed this feeling and began to focus on the work he had to finish so that he could get home to his woman.

CHAPTER SEVEN

The cobblestone streets of Germantown Avenue rattled the Jetta violently as Rafique headed to see his daughter. He had been spending a lot of time with his little girl since coming out of the hospital, and their relationship had improved dramatically.

A comfortable morning breeze kept the summer heat at a beautiful eighty degrees, perfect sunny conditions for a morning trip to the zoo. Coming close to her apartment, he slowed down to look for a parking spot. *Perfect, right in front of the house.* He pulled into the spot, turned the car off, and got out the car. Humming softly, he walked up to the two story apartment building and rang the bell. He didn't have to wait long before Veronica, his daughter's mother, called out from behind the closed door.

"Who is it?"

"It's me, Rafique." Slowly, the door swung open and Ronnie stood before him smiling.

"Hey, Rafique."

"What's up, where Tay at?"

"She's still at church with my mom. They should be back any minute. You want to come in and wait for them?"

"Yeah, I might as well."

Ronnie turned around and seductively strutted her way up the stairs to the second floor apartment.

"Damn, Ronnie! Is that all you?" He asked, entranced by the sway of her hips.

"Boy, stop playing, you know this is all me."

"What's up? I mean you alright? That nigga know what to do with all that?"

"Why, you think you can handle it?"

"Man, I handled it already, you know that."

"Are you sure about that?"

"Now you want to play. Hold up a minute, Ronnie." Rafique said, stopping in the middle of the stairway.

Ronnie stopped and faced him, "What you want?"

"Come here."

"No, Rafique, my man is upstairs."

"So what, come here."

"No boy, with your crazy ass," turning back around she continued up the stairs. Because Rafique had stepped up and began taking care of his responsibilities as a father, the relationship between he and Ronnie had improved for the better. So they jokingly went through this flirtatious sparing match every time they saw one another. Reaching the top of the stairway, Ronnie led Rafique into the kitchen.

"Ay, Ronnie, who was that at the door?" Her boyfriend called out from the living room.

"It's Shante's father!" She shouted back.

Rafique took a seat at the kitchen table and looked hungrily at Ronnie, "Yo, come here for a minute."

"No, Rafique, see I'm leaving your ass in here by yourself."

"Alright, just give me a quick kiss."

"Bye, Rafique," she said smiling as she began walking out of the kitchen.

"Hold up, Ronnie."

"What's up?"

"Can I use the phone?"

"Rafique, you ain't got to ask to use the phone."

"Naw, but I'm calling long distance."

"Go ahead, boy, don't be all long though."

"Alright, thanks, baby."

Ronnie smiled, slowly shaking her head, and left Rafique alone in the kitchen. Rafique laughed as he picked up the phone and began dialing the ten-digit number to Aisha's house in Washington, D.C.

✲ ✲ ✲

"Damn, Andre, ain't Rafique your boy?" Aisha asked sitting in her front room with the phone pressed tightly to her ear.

"Yeah, I mean we alright, but that don't change the fact that he neglecting you. Eesh, he really don't give a fuck about you. You just some easy, accessible, out of town pussy. How many times has he called you since he been out the hospital? How many times has he been to see you? Aisha, you deserve better than that. You need a nigga in your life that's gonna give you all the attention you deserve, all the love you need."

"And who might that be Andre, you?"

"Eesh it don't even matter who. What matters is that you get what you deserve. I wouldn't be real though if I sat up here and acted like I don't want it to be me, because I dig the shit out of you. You jive like the baddest shorty out Northwest and that's real rap. I'd be for you everything you need and then some."

Andre had been pursuing Aisha for months. Initially she rebuffed his advances with disdain but like a pack of African wild dogs, he was relentless with the pressure, feeding off her vulnerabilities, slowly chipping away at her defenses. With her man away for so long, the loneliness she felt opened her up to Andre's slick suggestions. She began to doubt Rafique's feelings towards her. *I do deserve better. Why should I be sitting around waiting for him? I'm nineteen. I ain't married. Fuck this, Rafique getting ready to blow.*

"Andre, I hear what you're saying, but Rafique is your friend. How would I look fucking with you?"

"Eesh, do it really matter who, I–,"

"Andre, hold on, that's my other line." Clicking over, she answered, "Hello."

"Eesh, what's up, baby?"

"Rafique, hold on," clicking back to Andre, Aisha lied, "Andre that's my mother on the other line. I'ma call you back."

"Alright, Eesh, don't forget, make sure you call me back."

"Alright, bye, Dre."

"Alright, Eesh."

Aisha clicked back to Rafique, her voice ice cold, "Yeah!"

"Damn, what's all that about? Fuck's up with your tone?"

"What you think it's about?"

"I don't know. What?"

"Rafique, I ain't seen you in months. I know you was in an accident and all that, but you could have at least called me since you've been home."

"I did call you. You ain't never the fuck home."

"When you call?"

"Man, I don't know."

"Look, Rafique, I can't be going through this. You suppose to be my man, but I ain't seen or heard from you in months. It's like I'm being faithful to a fucking ghost. It's like I ain't even got a man. So let me know right now. Do you want to be with me or what?"

"Eesh, I know I ain't been playing my part, but you got to understand how fucked up I was. I was in a coma for eight days. When I woke up I was delusional. I had a serious head injury and it took me this long just to get my bearings back. Look, man, I love you, and yeah, I still want to be with you. You still love me don't you?"

"Yeah, Rafique, I love you but it's been so hard. I miss you so much."

"I miss you too. As a matter of fact, I'm coming out there with my daughter at the end of the month."

"For real baby, I'll finally get a chance to meet your little girl?"

"Yeah."

"How long you staying for?"

"Just for the weekend, but I'll be back the following week."

"Excuse me, Rafique." Ronnie said interrupting his conversation.

"Rafique, who the fuck is that?" Aisha said, becoming angry.

"That's my daughter's mom."

"Oh."

"What's up, Ronnie?"

"My man getting ready to leave out and he don't feel comfortable with us being here alone."

"So what the fuck that mean?"

"Well, he don't want you here while he's gone."

"Are you out of your fucking mind!? I don't believe you even came to me with this shit! What the fuck is wrong with you!"

"Rafique, baby, calm down," Aisha said hearing the rage in her man's voice.

"Look, Eesh, I'ma call you back later on."

"Alright, baby, don't do nothing crazy."

"I ain't." Hanging up the phone, he turned his anger on Ronnie. "I ain't going nowhere!"

"So now what, you gonna fight him in your child's house? You gonna go through all that when you can just leave and come right back. Rafique that is my man. Why can't you just respect that?"

Rafique was silent for a moment trying to calm down so that he could think straight. Finally he answered, "Alright, look just tell my daughter I was here and I'll see her tomorrow."

"Rafique, why don't you just come back in like twenty minutes? Shante should be back any minute."

"Naw, it's cool. I got to go. I'm upset right now. So to avoid the dumb shit, I'm going to leave." He headed to the door with Ronnie trailing behind him.

On his way down the steps, Ronnie's man spoke to him. "Yo, my man – you ain't got to be talking to my woman all crazy like that either."

"What the fuck you say?"

"I said you ain't got to be talking to my girl like that."

Very upset now, Rafique turned to walk back up the stairs.

"No, Rafique, just go home. Don't listen to that shit. Please, Rafique, just leave."

Rafique stared hard at Ronnie and the pleading look in her eyes caused him to suck in his pride, turn and leave the apartment.

CHAPTER EIGHT

"Rafique!" Tracey shouted into the living room. "Huh!"

"Pick up the phone!"

Rafique reached over to the glass coffee table in front of the couch.

"Hello."

"What's up, cousin?"

"Damn, what's up, Mike?"

"Baby, you got it?" Tracey asked.

"Yeah, I got it." The phone clicked as Tracey hung up.

"What's up, Mike? Rafique asked as thoughts of Duck walking into his cell telling him that Mike was dead flashed through his mind. *It was only a dream,* he reminded himself.

"Yo, I was just calling to check up on you. You still be getting those headaches?"

"Yeah, but they ain't as bad as they were."

"That's what's up. You need anything?"

"Naw, I'm cool. I went out with Sean and them a couple of weeks ago and made me a nice piece of change."

"Well you know my offer still stands. I'm getting this money, man, and I could use somebody I can trust on my team."

"I'm cool, Mike, that Coke shit ain't my thing. I was thinking about fucking with Sean and his girl with that plastic though. I got to do something. This nut ass job I got ain't paying me shit. You know C.H. fucked up my weed pack. Tracey really been holding me down since I got out the hospital. This shit ain't me, man. I got to start holding my own weight. I mean when I went out with Sean and them that shit was so sweet. I think that's gonna be my new hustle."

"Yo, Fique, you know what, I almost forgot about this shit, too."

"What?"

"I got a piece of plastic in the mail yesterday, one of them MasterCard jawns. It's in a bitch name. Hold on a minute, while I go grab that jawn."

"Alright. Yo, Tracey, bring me a soda!" Rafique called out while waiting on Mike to come back to the phone.

"Yo, Fique, here it go right here. The bitch name is Lisa Cohen. They then sent this bitch shit to the wrong motherfucker. I was gonna give this to my young buck and tell him to just bring me back a few things. Fuck him though, you want it?"

"Yeah, fucking right."

"Alright, I got to go on the Southside in a few. I'ma drop it off on my way over there."

"Alright, that's what's up. Yo, you want me to pick you up something?"

"Naw, man, go ahead, get down, that's all you. You ain't got to give me shit. We family."

"Alright then, man, I'ma see you when you get here."

"Alright cuz, peace."

Rafique hung up the phone, picked it right back up and called Sean. The phone rang five times before Sean answered. "Hello."

"Sean, what's up man? What you doin today?"

"I'm getting ready to go out and get some money. Why, what's up?"

"Mike just called me. He got a MasterCard in the mail. It's in a bitch name though."

"Oh yeah."

"Yeah, he getting ready to bring it over in a few."

"So what's up, man? What you gonna do?"

"What you think? Why you think I'm calling you?"

"Oh alright, did he tell you the bitch name?"

"Yeah, it's, uh, Lisa Cohen."

"Alright, I'ma take Ari to go get some I.D. at Byron's and we'll be right over after that. Yo, we going out A.C."

"Whatever, man, I see you when you get here."

"Alright, man." Hanging up the phone Rafique got up and headed for the kitchen.

"Damn, Tray, what happened to the soda?"

"Oh, I'm sorry, baby. I got to breaking up these beans for our dinner tonight and forgot."

"Look, I'm getting ready to go out. I might be a little late tonight, so don't wait up for me."

"Where you going?"

"I'm going out A.C. with Sean and Ari."

"Can I go?"

"Naw, we going out there to take care of some business." Turning away from him she rolled her eyes and twisted her glossy thick lips into a pout.

Damn, she looked good when she's mad. "You mad at me?" He asked, smiling as he approached her.

"No, but baby, I just be wanting to be with you."

"Look, this business, seriously. I tell you what. We can go back out there this weekend, alright?"

Tracey smiled and nodded her head. Rafique leaned down and gently kissed her on her neck. "I love you," he whispered in her ear.

"I love you, too."

Rafique stood up, and left out the kitchen to go take a quick shower and to get dressed.

Rafique stepped into the Trump Plaza's Casino and was in awe of the lights. Dazzling, they gave the casino the facade of something heavenly. His first time on a casino floor, his head was on a swivel as he looked in one direction to the next absorbing everything he saw and heard, from the old ladies who had the slot machines on lock to the sudden shouts of joy coming from the crap tables, to the sullen looks of defeat from people who'd lost their weekly incomes. Cocktail waitresses carrying trays of watered down drinks, pranced around in next to nothing, attracting lustful stares and collecting big tips from high rollers with a need to impress. He smiled as he thought, *this shit is like a fantasy land.*

"Yo, Fique, come on, we going over to the five dollar black jack table." Sean said heading in that direction. Nodding his head, Rafique followed him.

A couple of hours earlier, as the sun slowly retreated behind the western horizon, Sean, Ari, and Rafique cruised down highway 42-East on the way to Atlantic City, N.J. Sitting in the back seat, Rafique stared absently at the cars that passed by and the trees that decorated the side of the highway. His mind was in overdrive as the two souls that were in constant battle raged a never ending war in his mind. *What the fuck are you doing, man? You acting like a blind man walking across a bridge full of holes. You know what living this kind of lifestyle can cost you. Is your freedom that expendable to you?*

Man, fuck all that, I need to get this money. What I'ma do? This is all I know – the fucking game. I can't have my woman taking care of me. I got to get this paper. Plus as long as I ain't hurting anybody, I'm cool.

Sean glanced at Rafique through the rearview mirror and interrupted his thoughts, "Ay, Fique, when we get there Ari gonna be on her own. Basically all we gonna be doing is wasting time until she finishes taking care of business. We just gonna play some low stakes, 21 or something, til she's ready, then we out."

"Alright, man, I'm with whatever. Let's just get this money," Rafique said as he turned his attention back to the highway. Now, as he followed Sean to the black jack table, he searched the floor for Ari. It didn't take him long to find her. Her long black hair cascaded luxuriously down her back. Her body, covered in a skintight Versace skirt, rivaled every woman in the casino as all eyes followed her hungrily. Six-inch cream-colored gator stilettos covered her petite feet as she strutted with confidence to a crap table.

The plan was for Ari to go to the cashier's window, and, using the credit card, get a cash advance, no more than $900. Anything more than a thousand would draw the manager. Once she received the cash she would then proceed to a table, play a few hands just for appearance sake and then it's off to the next casino to repeat the process. After Sean and Rafique played about ten hands of Black Jack and lost fifty dollars between the both of them, Sean spotted Ari leaving the casino. He tapped Rafique on the shoulder, and whispered in his ear, "Come on, let's get the fuck out of here."

Rafique picked up his last green chip and followed Sean towards the exit. He paused as he came upon a beautiful, dark-skinned cocktail waitress, and winked at her as he placed his last chip on her tray. She flashed him a radiant smile, winked back and watched him as he turned and walked out the casino. Once outside Sean turned to him and said, "Yo, why you give that broad twenty-five dollars?"

"Damn, that was twenty-five dollars?"

"Yeah, I told you the green ones was twenty-five."

"Maaannn, I thought you said they was five."

"Man, you knew it was twenty-five, trick ass nigga."

Laughing, Sean threw a playful jab at his homie.

"Yo, there's Ari right there," Sean said as he saw his girl walking towards them.

For the next few hours, the three friends played the casinos and collected money. Right before it was time for them to leave, they stopped at the Gucci Shop and did a little shopping. By the time they were finished, they had Gucci shopping bags full of clothing, ten thousand in cash, and a maxed out Mastercard.

Rafique was hooked. By the time they had arrived back in the city, his mind was made up. This would be his new hustle. For the next few weeks, he went out every day with Sean and Ari and every day they came up. When they weren't out playing, Sean got Rafique to practice on his pick-pocketing skills. After a couple of weeks, Rafique began to pull his own plastic while Sean and Ari did the blocking.

During this time, Fuzz called every day trying to get with Sean and Ari. The credit card game was how he was getting his money. Weeks had passed by since the last time he went out and he was almost broke. But every time he got in contact with Sean he was given one excuse after another about why he couldn't go. Finally, after weeks of ducking him and lying, Sean broke down and informed Fuzz that Rafique had been going out with them and that four people was one too many for the game that they were in. He thought that telling the truth was the right thing to do, so that Fuzz could move on to something else. Sean didn't think much else about it. What he didn't know, though, was that he had just poured gasoline over an already raging fire of jealousy that had engulfed his former partner.

CHAPTER NINE

WASHINGTON D.C.

Brightly colored leaves littered the pavement of 1st Street, a narrow residential street in the Northwest section of Washington DC. The skies, a depressing gray, were dotted with migratory birds as they took their annual flight south to escape the upcoming winter months. Pulling up on this block, Rafique turned to his daughter and said, "You nervous, Shante?"

"No," she responded as Rafique parked in front of his father's home.

"Well, we're here." Rafique turned the car off and he and his daughter got out. Minutes later, Rafique was knocking on his father's apartment door.

"Who is it?" a woman's voice answered the knock.

"It's Rafique."

The lock clicked and the door slowly swung open. Standing in the doorway, smiling warmly, was Lorraine. "Salam Alaikum, Rafique," she said, embracing her stepson.

"Wa Laikum As Salaam," Rafique responded.

She released her embrace and looked at Shante. "This must be Shante. How are you, beautiful? Looking just like your Dad. Come on in here and give your grandmother a hug."

Shante stepped inside the apartment slowly and wrapped her arms around her.

"Rafique! As salaam Alaikum. How are you, son?" Jamil said coming out of the bedroom.

"Wa Laikum Salaam, Abee. I'm cool."

"And this must be my granddaughter. Come here and let me look at you. Yea, you my granddaughter alright. Rafique, she looks just like you. Shante, how old are you now?"

"Six," Shante replied softly, her eyes glued to the floor.

"How was your trip?" Lorraine asked.

"Quick." Rafique responded.

"I know you wasn't speeding with my grandbaby in the car?" Lorraine asked giving Rafique a stern look.

"Naw, I wasn't speeding."

"Are you hungry, baby?" Lorraine asked Shante.

"No, my dad took me to McDonald's."

Jamil took a seat in his favorite chair and stared at his son and granddaughter beaming with pride. *Time waits for no man,* he thought. *It seems like only yesterday he was that size. Damn, I'm getting old.* "Rafique, your brother and sisters are on their way over here. I told them you were on your way with Shante, so they should be here any minute." As soon as those words escaped his mouth, the front door opened up and in walked Nafisah, Muhammad, and Najibah.

"Rafique!" Shouted Najibah as she sprinted over and embraced her big brother.

"Hey, Jibah, what's up?" Rafique said placing a kiss on her forehead.

"Nothing, I missed you."

"Say hi to your niece. Shante, this is your Aunt Najibah. Najibah, this is Shante."

"Hi, Aunt Najibah."

"Just call me Jibah. You ain't got to call me Aunt Najibah. How you doing, Shante?

"Fine."

"Shante, this is your Aunt Nafisah and your Uncle Muhammad." One after the other, Nafisah and Muhammad introduced themselves to Shante. As Shante got acquainted with the family, Rafique slipped away into the bedroom to use the phone. He was back in DC and he had to call his baby.

☆ ☆ ☆

Aisha sat alone in her apartment with her favorite Go-Go Band, Rare Essence, blasting from the twelve-inch woofers she had placed strategically around her house. The pounding of the African Congas had the paper thin walls of the apartment shaking as she nodded her head to the beat. With the ancient African rhythms pulsating throughout her body, her mind occupied, she couldn't stop thinking about Andre. He had been steadily increasing the pressure and her will was beginning to crack. *Andre right, I'm nineteen years old and I look good as shit. I can have any nigga I want, and I'm sitting around here waiting on a nigga that live hundreds miles away, who only comes to see me once in a blue moon. Fuck this; it's time for me to move on. That dick ain't all that good... Is that my phone ringing?* She walked back to the couch, reached over to the coffee table and picked up the phone. "Hello."

"Damn, girl, what took you so long to pick up the phone?"

"Rafique?"

"Yeah, what's up?"

"Where you at?"

"I'm around the corner."

"For real?"

"Yeah, me and my little girl just got in town."

"When you comin to see me?"

"I'll be there in a few minutes."

"You bringing your daughter with you?"

"Naw, not today, she with the family right now. You'll meet her tomorrow."

"Alright, make sure you bring her. I told you I wanted to meet her."

"Ok, I'll bring her. What's up, though, you miss me?"

"Yeah, I miss you, but Rafique we need to talk."

"What's up?"

"Not over the phone. I'll see you when you get here."

"Ok, give me an hour or two. Get dressed, too. We're going out."

"Where we going?"

"Where you want to go?"

"I don't really feel like nothing extravagant. Let's just go down Union Station and go to the movies or something."

"Alright, if that's what you…"

"Hold on a minute, Rafique, somebody is on my other line." Clicking over, she answered the other line. "Hello."

"What's up, Aisha?"

"Andre?"

"Yeah, what's up?"

"You gonna have to call me back. Rafique's on the other line."

"Look at you, easy access."

"Dre, I'll call you back."

"Yeah, alright."

"Rafique," she said clicking back to him.

"Yeah, who was that?"

"That was my girlfriend Peaches."

"Ok, well look, you can go ahead and call her back. I'm going to spend a little time with my folks and then I'll be around there."

"Alright, baby, I love you."

"I love you, too."

Aisha hung up the phone, got up and walked to the bathroom. All the frustration of being alone was now gone. Her man was in town and he would be there soon. That was all that mattered. She turned on the shower and got undressed. She had to get ready. She wanted to look and smell extra good when he arrived.

✷ ✷ ✷

Street lamps lit up the nighttime skies in an artificial glow as Rafique and Aisha cruised down the Washington D.C. streets. Conversation was light as they mostly listened to soft music blaring from the car speakers. Aisha stared at her man and felt confused. She loved him, but she felt so lonely. She use to think she could handle a long distance relationship, but that was when he was coming to see her every weekend. Ever since his accident, though, the time they spent together was virtually non-existent. On top of all that, she had to deal with the constant pressure Andre had been putting on her. Everything he said seemed to be on point. So she had to get some answers. She needed to know if Rafique was really going to be with her or not. If he said he wanted to, then she needed to be reassured that he would step up. She was tired of feeling so lonely.

"THIS IS WPGC AND TONIGHT'S TOPIC IS AIDS AND HOW IT'S AFFECTING THE BLACK COMMUNITY. OUR PHONE LINES ARE OPEN AND WE'RE WAITING ON YOUR CALLS."

Aisha reached over and began turning the station.

"Eesh, turn that back, I want to hear that."

"I want to hear some music, baby. I don't want to listen to that depressing ass shit."

"Alright, just turn back for a minute."

She sucked her teeth and turned back. Just as she reached the station, they were just receiving their first call.

"Hello, I'm calling about today's topic on the AIDS thing."

"What's your name caller?"

"My name is Cherry."

"Ok, Cherry, say what's on your mind?"

"Well, about three months ago I was diagnosed with HIV."

"I'm sorry to hear that, Cherry. How have you been making out?"

"Well, when I first found out, I was devastated. I mean, I didn't even want to live any more. But then I got angry and that anger fueled my desire to live and ever since then I've been making them pay."

"Making who pay, Cherry?"

"Every mother (beep) that was born with a (beep)."

"Oh shit, Eesh, you hear that?" Rafique asked.

"Ssshhhh," Aisha said totally caught up in the conversation taking place on the radio.

"Cherry, why would you want to put someone else through all the pain you went through? These people you're talking about are innocent."

"They aren't innocent. They shouldn't be so eager to be (beep) without a condom. That's how I got it, one of them nasty (beep) (beep) ain't care about what they was giving to me, so now I don't care. Look, I have been on this phone too long. You might be trying to trace it or something. I'm out.

"Cherry, Cherry, ladies and gentlemen if you were listening to that conversation, it was real. This was not something our radio station cooked up to scare people. Cherry is a real person and I believe she means what she said. So all you brothers out there you have to be careful, cause Cherry could be someone you know. And, Cherry, if you're still listening, please sweetheart, re-think what you're doing. Don't take out what some jive dude did to you on some undeserving brother. I'm sorry, but we have to take a break right now. We'll be back with more on this explosive topic."

"Yo, turn that off, Eesh. Put in my Guy tape."

"Oh, so now you don't want to listen to it. You see, that's what them dirty dick motherfuckers get."

"Damn, Eesh, what kind of shit is that to say?"

"Fuck em, they want to be running around fucking everything that move, that's what they get."

"Yeah, well, they can't fuck by themselves. Sis mad at the wrong person, she should be mad at herself. Nobody made her fuck without a condom."

"How you know, Rafique? She could've been raped."

"Man, she wasn't raped. If she was, she would have said that. She just wants to run around and blame everybody else for her fucked up choices."

"Well, what if she was being faithful and her man gave it to her?"

"Fuck all that 'if' shit. We just got to go by what she said, and she ain't say none of that shit. She probably picked a nigga up at the club, took him home, and fucked him. However she got it don't justify what she's doing now. I'm telling you, if you ever cheat on me and bring me back something..."

"Nigga, you the one probably fucking somebody. Cause you damn sure ain't been fucking me. That's probably why it took you so long to come out here. I know you probably got a bitch out in Philly. That's why I ain't been out there yet. Can you answer that? How come you've never taken me to Philly, Rafique, huh?"

"What the fuck is this? Where is all this coming from? You think I got somebody else? Is this what you wanted to talk to me about? Aisha, I was in the hospital. I was in a fucking coma. I almost died. Everything ain't always about you all the time. You know, that's the only reason why I ain't been out here. What, you've been listening to one of these niggas out here or something? You let one of these nut ass niggas fill your head with some bullshit. Look, Eesh, I love the shit out of you, but if you can't trust me, there's no need for us to be together. Is that what you want?"

Aisha was silent as tears began streaming down her face. Choking back the sobs, she responded, "Rafique, I love you too, but it's just been so hard on me not having you around for months. Every time I call you mother's house, you're never there. I can't help but feel insecure. I know that you were hurt real bad and I'm sorry, baby, but it's just been so hard on me. I've been so lonely Rafique and I don't feel like I should be feeling this way if I got a man."

Rafique pulled over and looked at her. "Look at me, Eesh. I'm sorry if I made you feel like that. I'm completely healthy now and I promise you that things are gonna get back to how they were. Plus, you can come to Philly next week to meet my mom and them, alright. I love you, man, and I always want you to be a part of my life. You okay?"

Slowly nodding her head, she wiped the tears from her eyes, "You promise?"

"Yeah, I promise." Rafique replied before he leaned over and kissed her passionately.

Aisha came up for air and looked him in the eye. "I love you so much, Rafique."

"I love you too, baby." With that said, Rafique put the car back in drive and pulled off.

☼ ☼ ☼

Union Station was jam-packed on this Friday night as Rafique and Aisha arrived. The newly renovated train station was a weekend hot spot. No longer just a train station, it was a combination between a train station and a mall. Full of clothing and jewelry shops, a food court, one of the hottest bars in town and a state of the art multiplex movie theatre, it was the place to be for politicians, tourists, and locals looking to get out and enjoy themselves after a stressful work week.

Hand in hand, they strolled through the crowded walkway on the way to the movies. The outward display of public affection he was showing was a little reassuring to her, easing her insecurities some, causing her to squeeze his hand. Rafique felt her grip tighten, and looked at her and smiled. She matched his stare and smiled before speaking. "This is a surprise, holding hands in public? You must be feeling real sentimental."

He chuckled, "Damn, what you embarrassed? You want me to let go of your hand?"

"No, I'm just saying you don't usually do this. It caught me off guard a little bit. I like it, though. It's reassuring to know that you love me enough to not be afraid to show it in front of people."

"You're my, baby, man I should have been doing this kind of shit a long time ago. Maybe if I had, you wouldn't be feeling like you were feeling. You know, with the doubts and all that. But like I said, from here on out, shit gonna be different. You ain't never gonna have a reason to doubt me again."

His words were exactly the thing she needed to hear. All the doubt, frustration, loneliness, and insecurities began to melt away. If the late great famous photographer, Gordon Parks, was commissioned to take a picture of something beautiful to grace the cover of a magazine, the smile of happiness and contentment that lit up her face would have been a perfect model of beauty to capture in one of his still frames.

As they continued to stroll hand in hand through the mall, loud pop music could be heard in the distance.

"What the fuck is that? They got a club in here now or something?" Rafique asked as the music became louder.

"No, you know Fat Tuesdays is right up ahead of us. It's Friday and the white folks is letting their hair down."

"Oh yeah, come on, we going in that jawn."

"No, Rafique, I don't want to go in there with all those white people. I want to go the movies," Aisha replied pouting.

"Come on with the sad, sexy look. I only want to stop in there for a minute."

She sucked her teeth but relented just as the bar came into view.

"Damn, this motherfucker jam-packed," Rafique said looking inside at the standing room only crowd. "Come on, baby, real quick." Rafique led the way, maneuvering their way inside the bar and through the crowd.

The music was deafening and the crowded dance floor was full of bodies void of rhythm, moving as if they were dancing to the words of the song instead of the beat. *Damn, I thought I couldn't dance. These motherfuckers are ridiculous.* Rafique thought as he continued to walk towards the bar. As soon as he reached the bar, he spotted his target. Rafique leaned over and whispered in Aisha's ear, "Eesh, I need you to stand directly behind my right shoulder."

With a look of confusion, Aisha nodded her head. Intoxicated bar patrons paid them no mind as Rafique slid in next to his victim, ordered a soda, and waited for Aisha to block the view of his right arm. With her expensive Coach ban hanging loosely off of her left shoulder, Rafique's victim was unaware as he sat his drink on the bar and went to work. He unzipped her bag expertly, removed her wallet, extracted her Visa, placed the wallet with her money untouched back into her bag, and zipped it back up. As cool and calm as a con man running game, he then turned and winked at Aisha and said, "Come on, Eesh, we out." He grabbed her hand and led the way back through the non-dancing crowded dance floor and out of the bar.

"That's all you wanted to go in there for was a soda? You could have gotten one at the movies."

"That's not what I went in there for. Look." Pulling out the Visa, he showed it to Aisha.

"Baby, where did you get that, you found it?" Chuckling, he nodded his head.

"Yo, we gonna go use this jawn right now."

"Baby, how we gonna use that? Look at the name."

Rafique looked down at the name, Susan Bradkowsky. *Damn, this might be a problem.*

"Eesh, is there a store in here that got some young black people working behind the counter?"

"Yeah, it's a store upstairs called Urban Wear."

"Alright, come on, that's where we're going."

Rafique took a quick look around Urban Wear, searching for someone he could step to about the credit card. His eyes slowly zoned in on the front counter and became frozen there. From the back she was built like an African Goddess. A small waist line opened up into curvaceous hips connected to the phattest ass he had ever seen. At that same instant, she turned around. His heart hammered in his chest while his stomach did back flips. *This can't be; I got to be losing my mind. What the fuck is this? It's Monique from my dream.*

"Baby, why you staring at that girl like that? Are you okay? Your face is covered in sweat. What's wrong?"

Aisha's voice snapped Rafique from his thoughts. He wiped the sweat from his brow. "I'm cool, Eesh, I just got one of those headaches I be getting. I'll be okay in a minute. Look, let me holla at sis. Go start picking stuff out. Don't worry about the cost either."

"What do you mean, 'let you go holla at sis'? Are you crazy? What you got to holla at her about?"

"Eesh, how else we gonna use a card with a name like Bradkowski on it? I got to go see if sis is cool, and whether or not she'll take a couple of dollars to let us use it."

Aisha felt a little self-conscious about her pang of jealously and flashed an embarrassed smile before walking away to pick out some clothes.

With Aisha out of the way, he approached the counter. His heart still beating hard, he tried to relax, to no avail. Sweat beads formed on his forehead again, as his stomach continued to flip violently. He reached the counter and looked at her nametag. M. Thompson. In a mild state of shock, he continued to stare.

"Um, excuse me, can I help you?" the girl behind the counter asked as she stared back at Rafique with an attitude.

"Oh, damn, my fault. But is your name Monique?"

She paused for a moment giving his question some thought. "How do you know my name?"

What the fuck, it is her. He suppressed the feelings of shock and went on automatic pilot as the words poured out of him. "You probably don't remember me, but I was in your first grade class."

Once again she paused before answering as she pondered what he said. "Yeah, you right. I don't remember you. But how you remember me from all those years ago?"

"You never forget your first love. I used to have a serious crush on you, but back then I was scared of girls. I was real shy."

"Are you still scared of girls?" She asked smiling. "Do you still have a crush on me?"

He returned her smile with one of his own. "To your first question, naw, I ain't scared no more, and to your second question, believe it or not, yeah."

"Well, that's a good thing."

"Is it?"

"Yeah."

As Monique and Rafique continued to talk, Aisha couldn't focus on what she was doing. She was so worried about the conversation her man was having with the clerk. *Why is that bitch all smiling in my man's face? What the fuck is he saying to her? No, see, she smiling too hard for this to be about some credit card shit.* Still acting as if she was picking out clothes, she eased closer to see if she could catch a little of their conversation.

"Damn, let me apologize. I didn't even introduce myself. Since you don't remember me, my name is Rafique."

"Rafique, huh? Well, Rafique, where you from? Cause I can tell from the way you talk, that you're not from around here."

"Yeah, I'm from Philly. I got family here, though."

"How long you in town for?"

"I'm only here until Sunday." Looking up at the big round mirror hanging up high behind the counter, Rafique spotted Aisha creeping up behind him acting as if she was looking at clothes. "Listen, Monique, I'm here with my friend, so I can't holla at you right now. Are you going to be here tomorrow?"

"Yeah."

"What time you get off?"

"I get off at six."

"Alright, I'ma stop by then to pick you up so we can talk some more. As a matter of fact, we're going out to eat. But look, I got a proposition for you."

"What's up?"

"I got a credit card I just found and I want to use it. If you're down, I'll give you a hundred to let me use it here."

"Shit, I don't care. Ain't none of this shit mine." Rafique dug in his pocket, pulled out the money and paid her. After seeing the money transaction, Aisha felt a lot better.

"Alright, look, Monique, I'ma holla at you tomorrow. Let me go ahead and get this shit out the way before my friend starts tripping."

"Alright, make sure you come back tomorrow."

"Rest assured, I'm definitely coming back." With that said he gave her a wink and walked away. *This is the second time a motherfucker from my dream has popped up in real life. What the fuck is happening to me?*

"It took you long enough. You better not had been over there flirting with that bitch." Aisha said as Rafique rejoined her.

"Eesh, I ain't gonna lie, I did do a little flirting but it worked. We can use the card. It cost me a couple of dollars, but it's gonna be worth it."

"Alright then, let's go shopping, everything on Susan Bradkowski." Aisha said as she began picking out the most expensive things in the store.

CHAPTER TEN

♫ *Slowly, MY EYEEESS BEGAN TO SEE*
THAT I NEED YOU HERE,
RIGHT WITH ME,
AT ALL TIMES ♫

As Wanya Morris of Boyz II Men belted out the first verse of their single, Please Don't Go, Rafique watched Aisha slowly get undressed. Seductively, she swayed her hips to the rhythm of the song as she unbuttoned, unzipped, and provocatively eased her pink Polo sweatpants down to her ankles. She stepped out of them, and her eyes never left his as she enticingly bit her bottom lip. As he became aroused, his blood pressure rose and his heart rate quickened in anticipation. Aisha pulled her tee shirt over her head, tossed it to the side, and stood with her knees locked back and her hands on her hips at the foot of the bed.

A strange sense of déjà vu flooded his being as he approached her. He couldn't help but think of his dream and a similar situation. The same song was playing, the same black satin sheets covered the bed, the same glow from the same scented candles illuminated the room, and the same picture of womanly perfection stood waiting for him. He shook all thoughts of his dream and weird feelings of déjà vu from his mind and continued to walk towards her, stopping only when his chest grazed her erect nipples. Rafique pulled her close, pressing her soft body against his own. He could feel the rhythm of her heartbeat as it pounded in her chest. Gently but firmly, he gripped her ponytail and tilted her head back. With her neck exposed, he began sucking on it.

"Uummm," she moaned as she reached down and began rubbing his dick. He moved from her neck and kissed her flush on the mouth. As their tongues danced, he released the grip he had on her hair and let his hands explore the rest of her body. Rafique knew all of her hot spots, so he touched, licked and sucked, raising the sexual tension to an unbearable peak. He stopped suddenly, stepped back and removed his Fila sweat suit, tee shirt and silk boxers. Naked except for his ankle socks, he approached as she removed her matching bra and panties. Aisha retreated onto the bed and backed up to the headboard, opened her legs wide, licked her bottom lip and stared at him invitingly. He followed her, crawling across the bed and coming to a stop on his knees in between her legs. Slowly he began kissing her again. He started from her forehead and moved to her full lips, parting them, tasting her tongue. From her mouth he moved to her neck, sucking, not too hard, but just right. From her neck he kissed a trail to her breast.

"Uummm," she cooed in his ear as he moved from breast to breast gently licking and sucking, driving her wild with sexual intoxication.

Their body temperatures rose as sweat, the body's natural coolant, began to form. Without pause, Rafique's tongue moved from her breast leaving a wet trail down her stomach. He continued on until he reached the softest place on earth.

"Oh my god," she cried out as his tongue did an exotic dance with her clitoris. Slowly she began grinding her hips as her hands gripped his head tight. "It feels sooo good," she purred child-like as he inserted his finger activating her g-spot. Her cries of pleasure became constant as he kept up the pressure, licking, sucking, and probing.

"I'm getting ready to cum!" she shouted, grinding her hips furiously. Without warning he stopped and looked up from in between her legs. Her juices shined off of his lips, glistening like lip gloss, as he smiled. "Not yet, you got to wait for me."

"You want to cum too, baby?" she asked, her eyes clouded over with lust. "Lay on your back," she instructed as she moved over to allow him to switch position. Without hesitation, she went to work, hovering over him, she began kissing him passionately, tasting her own juices that still covered his lips. Quickly she moved to his chest, sucking his nipples hard, causing him to moan with pleasure. Pausing there for only a second, she too left a wet trail down his body coming to a stop when she reached his throbbing manhood. Gripping it in her hand, she expertly began massaging it before inserting it into her mouth. Her hands and mouth working in tandem had him moaning in pleasure. "God damn, girl, this shit feel good."

"You like it, baby?" she asked looking him in the eye.

"Yeah, I like it, ssss, uuhh."

"Tell me when you're ready to cum."

"I'm ready to cum now."

Releasing him, she got up and straddled him. Grabbing his dick, she guided him inside her. Slowly they developed a rhythm, moving their bodies as if they were one. Becoming lost in their combined rhythms, all that existed for them was the pleasure that enveloped them, mind, body, and soul, until they both exploded in orgasmic ecstasy.

Rolling off him, she snuggled close, laying her head on his chest. "Rafique, I love you so much," she said listening to the rhythm of his pounding heart.

"I love you too, man," he responded. "Ay, Eesh, you know I can't stay."

"Why not?"

"Cause my daughter is at my pop's house. I can't stay out all night and leave her there like that."

"When you leaving?"

"I don't know. I'll probably wait til you go to sleep. I'll be back first thing in the morning with my little girl so you can meet her. It'll be like I didn't even leave."

Satisfied, Aisha relaxed and closed her eyes. Moments later they both drifted off to sleep.

KNOCK…KNOCK…KNOCK…KNOCK

Loud knocking on the door woke Rafique out of his sleep. *Who the fuck is this knocking on the door like that?* He sat up groggily in the bed and looked at Aisha sleeping peacefully. *Damn, she sleeps through anything.* Getting up, he stumbled blindly through the dark bedroom and into the hallway. Rafique turned on the light switch and illumination corrupted the blackness flooding the hallway as he walked to the front door.

KNOCK…KNOCK…KNOCK…KNOCK

"Who the fuck is it?!" He shouted, opening the door at the same time.

"Where's that bitch at?"

"Tracey? How the fuck- what you doing out here?" His heart pounding in his chest, Rafique stared in shock at his girl from Philly who stood in the doorway of his girl in DC.

"Rafique who's that at my door this time of night?" Aisha called out. The last knocks must have awakened her.

"I knew you had a bitch in there!" Tracey said as she pushed her way past him.

Rafique jumped up, his face bathed in sweat, and looked around the dark bedroom. *Oh shit, it was just a dream.* Swinging his legs over the side of the bed, he wiped the sweat off his brow, and looked at Aisha. *Damn I love this girl, but Tracey is my baby too. I love em both for different reasons. What one doesn't have, the other one does. I'm glad they live in two different cities, cause if they were both in Philly, I don't know what I'd do.* He eased out of the bed so as not to awaken her, picked up his clothes, got dressed and made his way out of the apartment.

* * *

Fifteen minutes later Rafique pulled up on 1st Street and slowly cruised down the block searching for a parking spot.

"Yo, Fique!" He looked in the direction he heard his name being called and saw Dre walking towards the car.

"Hold up, Dre, let me park!" He found a spot, parked and got out of the car.

"What's up, Dre?"

"What's up, Fique?" Dre responded, embracing Rafique.

"What you doing, man?"

"I just came from around on Gallatin Street. These niggas from New York just set up shop around there. You know me, I been getting cool with them niggas so I can rob their bama asses."

"Oh yeah, what's up with em?"

"They sweet, that's what's up with em. I been smoking a little weed with em for the past couple months and these stupid ass bamas let me see everything I need to see."

"Are they strapped?" Rafique asked as that strange sense of déjà vu flooded his being again. *I can't believe this shit. I had this same conversation with him in my dream. If he say they keep their guns in the bedroom, I might be really losing my fucking mind.*

"Yeah, they're strapped, but these bama ass niggas be keeping the guns in the bedroom." Rafique was now in a daze, swamped in total confusion. With a blank look in his eyes, he stared at Andre.

"Yo, Fique, what's up man?"

"Huh, oh damn, my fault. I zoned out for a minute. I be getting like that sometimes from the accident." Rafique said. Not wanting to sound crazy, he kept his constant flashes of déjà vu to himself.

"So, what's up man, you want to get these niggas or what?"

Graterford's cold, drab, forty foot razor wire topped wall flashed through his mind as he pondered Dre's request. "Naw, man, I'm cool. I got my little girl out here with me and between spending time with the family and Aisha, I ain't got the time for nothing else."

Pangs of jealously ripped through Andre's body at the mention of Aisha's name. He camouflaged this envy and just smiled as Rafique continued. "Plus, I'm cool on the paper side. What's up with you? You alright?"

"Naw, I'm fucked up youngin. That's why I got to rob these niggas."

Pulling his money out, Rafique handed Dre two fifty dollar bills. "Like I said, I'm cool. Take this so you can have a little something in your pocket." "Damn, good looking out, youngin. I needed this. I'm still gonna take them bamas shit, though. I'll get Qua to go with me."

"Qua, huh?" Qua getting ready to get a rape during the robbery in his dream flashed through Rafique's mind. "Ay, Dre, I know Qua your man and what not, but if you take him with you, you better keep an eye on him. I'm telling you he's liable to turn a simple robbery into some other shit."

"Why you say that?"

Again, not wanting to reveal that he got his information from a dream and not wanting to run the risk of sounding crazy, Rafique simply said, "Come on man, you know that nigga ain't bright."

Dre chuckled and nodded his head. "Yeah, youngin, you right. That nigga is dumb as a motherfucker."

"Look, Dre, I got to go man. My pop is probably in there bitching. I left my daughter there hours ago."

"Alright then, youngin, be cool."

"Alright, Dre, I'll holla at you tomorrow." Shaking Andre's hand, Rafique turned and headed up the steps to his father's apartment.

CHAPTER ELEVEN

After knocking, Rafique stared at the designs the peeling paint made on the hallway ceiling as he waited patiently for someone to answer his father's front door. Moments later the door slowly swung open with Jamil standing there, smiling warmly.

"Salaam Alaikum, Rafique. I've been waiting up for you so that we can make salaat (prayer) together."

"I'm cool, Abbee. I'm real tired and I just want to go lay on that couch and go to sleep."

Worry lines creased his father's forehead in irritation as he responded, "What do you mean, you don't feel like it? This ain't no request."

"Look, Abbee, no disrespect, but I'm a grown ass man." Rafique knew that this day was coming. Ever since he woke up from the coma, he had been feeling differently about a lot of things and religion was one of those things. He knew he had to have this conversation with his father, although he dreaded it. Rafique closed the door behind him and began pacing slowly around the living room. Jamil watched his son and wondered what this was all about.

"Rafique, what's up with you? Where's all this coming from?"

"Abbee, don't take this the wrong way, but I ain't that naïve little boy who's afraid to express how he feels. I've changed, man, and I think it's time for us to talk because if you don't look at me for who and what I am, a grown ass black man, we'll never be able to relate as we should. Instead of you respecting my intelligence and the fact that I'm a man who thinks freely and who has beliefs that are different from yours, you'll continue to perceive me as this confused son who only needs the wise guidance of his father. Don't get me wrong, I still welcome your insights because I understand that you know a lot more than I do. But that doesn't mean that I'll take what you say as law. You see, I understand a lot of what you say is based on what you believe. I've learned through reading about our history that the ancient Kemetians taught that knowing must be the basis of faith, not believing. For believing is for those who do not know."

Jamil smiled as he pulled out his Marlboro Lights and lit one up. Taking a deep drag, he slowly exhaled the pale smoke into the air as he shifted positions in his favorite chair. He plucked the ashes off into the ashtray as he responded, "You know, Rafique, what's most interesting about what you just expressed is the fact that in expressing yourself, you've demonstrated an intellectual ability I've been waiting many years to see. But first and foremost, let me say this. If you wouldn't have been born black, I wouldn't have recognized you as my son. I assume, though, you're referring to your politics. My politics are not so much different from yours as you may think. I've known you were a man for a very long time and I've waited for a long time for you to know it. I will admit, though, that for a long time I have perceived you in the exact same way you've understood, as my confused son in need of guidance from his father. But you must admit, my assessment at the time was not wrong. Times change, Rafique, and I realized that you had changed when I talked to you on the phone after you came out of the coma. If you think I haven't dealt with you since then in a way that demonstrated my knowledge of who you are, it is only because over the years you've refused to act like who you are. I mean, I couldn't get you to say more than two words to me at a time. So right now, hearing you express yourself in the manner that you have, has me nervous with anticipation. I mean, finally my son is presenting a challenge to me."

He paused in his pacing and looked at his father. He then resumed his pacing and responded, "Abbee, I'm really having a problem with religion right now."

"A problem with religion, for what?"

"It's the dream I had…"

"A dream? How can you come to me about religion from…?"

"Hold up, hold up, my fault. Forget I said something about a dream. I've been thinking about this for a while now. My problem is every religion says their way is the right way and you have millions of people who believe that their religion is the chosen one, and they base this on faith. But what do they base their faith on? I mean, how do we know that Jesus actually died on a cross and then was resurrected? How do we know that the Prophet Muhammad didn't come off that mountain with Hebrew stories he memorized from Waraka ben Naufal? How do we know if he was motivated not by revelation, but by the need to obtain power? I'm not trying to make a mockery; I'm simply trying to make a point. Point being, there's no way of knowing. That's where faith comes in at. Now what is that faith based on? Knowing or belief? The way I feel right now, I don't think I can ever become involved in another religion because I believe it's used as a tool to divide, pacify, and to keep the oppressed peoples of the world in their same fucked-up positions – looking for a better day, once they die. I mean, you got brothers running around calling each other kaffirs. Yeah, the same name the racist whites in South Africa use to demean the Africans. This is a classic example of dividing a people that should otherwise be united for their very survival. When these white folks look at us they don't see a Muslim or a Christian, they see niggers." Suddenly he stopped his pacing and took a seat on the couch facing his father. Rafique pulled out a pack of Newports, extracted one and lit it up while waiting on his father to respond.

Jamil calmly took another drag from his cigarette, stubbed it out and handed the ashtray to Rafique. He cleared his throat. "Rafique, don't assume anything about people, especially about me. Why do you think that I have imposed on you a belief that I have which has no basis in fact? Why do you place me in the same category as Chauvin, who followed Napoleon to war because of his blind faith in him? As I am sure you are aware, the word chauvinist, a blind follower, is taken from his behavior. Rafique, as you should know, I was raised in a Methodist Church. My mother told me about Islam when I was fifteen years old. I didn't accept it until I was twenty-one. I've studied Swahili before I studied Arabic. My name was Msonge before it was Jamil and my heroes are Chaka Zulu, Osei Tutu, Nandi, Melik II and many more from Africa. Malcolm X, H. Rap Brown, Stokely Carmichael...I could go on and on naming people, places and events that surround my evolution. But, the point is, Islam didn't just jump on me. I had to study. I'm still to this day concerned with the upliftment of my people. That's why I got into drug counseling. So, for you to say what you're saying, indicates to me that you really don't know who you are. We are alike in many ways,

Rafique. To know me is to know yourself. Yes, you are an individual who thinks for himself, but so am I. I didn't expect you to accept what I say as law just because I said it. I'm not Christian today, not because I was rebellious and not because of my mother. My mother wanted me to be Muslim because she loved Malcolm. But she wasn't Muslim and didn't become one until long after I did. I became Muslim after investigating a lot of other religions, and seeing that most Christians couldn't answer the hard questions. I had to study it. You say knowing must be the basis of faith. To a degree, I agree. That's one of the reasons man is distinct from other animals. His ability to reason, his ability to know. It is said that none worship Allah better than the learned. Faith and belief are almost the same in the English language. If you look up one, it's defined by the other. When you utilize the term creation, you are presupposing a creator. Under the circumstances this does not prove the existence of a Supreme Being. In view of the fact that language, culture and religion are often times interconnected, you cannot prove that there is a creator just because you use these terms. You've only proved that you believe in the existence of a creator. Faith is not necessarily, in this case especially, based on knowing that which can be proved, nor for that matter disproved. If you use the term 'evolve' instead of 'create,' it puts another spin on the whole subject, doesn't it?"

Rafique slowly nodded his head.

"The question of Muhammad memorizing Hebrew stores from Waraka Ben Nufail is an interesting one, but indeed I would think that the Quran as regards to these Hebrew stories would say the same thing as the Bible. Waraka Ben Nufail was an old man. He died soon after meeting Muhammad. But this is not proof. It's up to you whether or not you want to believe it."

Blowing smoke rings in the dimly lit front room, Rafique narrowed his already slanted eyes and stared at his father. "Abbee, I hear you, but it's still a lot of things that just don't make sense. Like why do we allow the historical and contemporary enemies of our people to control and influence our lives? In fact, virtually all of the information that governs our lives is from people who hate us the most. From the languages we speak to the religions we practice. You speak Arabic fluently, but that ain't your language. When you traveled the world, did you think to try to find out where you came from, your family name or the original language of your people, or who those people were? I doubt it. You were probably over seas rubbing elbows with those Arabs. The same Arabs that are enslaving Africans to this day."

"Were you listening to me, son? You didn't hear me when I said I studied Swahili? There's obviously a lot of things that you don't know. Like the fact that there are two kinds of Arabs. But before I get into that, I must tell you that the term Arab is from the root word Araba, which meant Swift River in its early translation. Clear speech is its more current meaning. It applied specifically to language. When Muhammad was asked who is the Arab? He replied, 'The Arab, it is the tongue.' Each tribe during the earlier times were known and identified by their tribal names. An example of this would be the tribe of Sunni Hashim or Hashemite. There is also the clan of Quarish. These designations existed until World War I, when a British Intelligence Officer, known as Lawrence of Arabia, influenced the onset of Arab nationalism to unite an otherwise disunified people against the Ottoman Turks, who at that time were allied with the Germans; who under General Bismarck fought the British and French over the carving up and colonization of Africa." Pausing for a moment, Jamil yawned before continuing. "Damn, I'm getting tired.

Anyway, the two kinds of Arabs, one is called Assyria. Their language was Syriac. They became arabized and now are considered Arabs. These are the fair skinned ones. They come from what was once called Assyria. The second group are called Quahatani. They come from the southern tip of the Arabian Peninsula. These are the original Arabs, the descendants of the Ad and Thamud people mentioned in the Qur'an. These people are Black. My reason for bringing this to your attention is because you're obviously not aware of the fact that Arabia is and always has been a part of Africa geographically. In 1869, the Suez Canal was built separating a land mass and joining the Red Sea to the Mediterranean Sea. Prior to this time, the separated land mass was previously an often used land bridge that extended from Africa to an area once known as Paran. Today this area once known as Paran is called Arabia. Now, a continent is a great division of land surrounded by water. Prior to 1869, Africa and Arabia were joined. You say Arabic is not my language. This you cannot prove by any stretch of the imagination. I guess Hebrew is not my language either or Aramaic. Don't assume where our roots are from Rafique. Africa is very large and it's people and languages numerous. Are you following me?" Rafique nodded his head.

"You made the statement that religion is used to divide. In my view, religion brings people together. Democracy is a religion, monarchies are a religion. My point is, your understanding of religion will be as narrow as your definition of it. I define it as, lifestyles or a way of living. It encompasses a common culture which includes language, rules of behavior and a political agenda. Surely Allah didn't just put us here and say go for self. I know you can imagine what the result of that would be. Rafique you are my right side. Why do you feel the need to move from my side? Why are you rejecting what you are for some vague notion of Nationalism or Pan Africanism?"

Stubbing out his cigarette Rafique raising his voice slightly asked, "Why do you feel like I've left your side? Why do you feel like this? Is it because I've finally used the ability to think that God has blessed me with? An ability that you helped me discover. Because I question you about your beliefs, you feel like I'm not with you anymore? I haven't left your side. I'm just questioning things that don't make sense to me. Keep in mind that this is man to man. So please don't give me religious dogma or the father knows best attitude. My goal is not to prove you wrong, it's just to share with you how I think and to discover the truth. This way, maybe both of us can come to an understanding and you won't pressure me into something that I'm not sure about. You asked me why do I reject again who and what I am for some vague notion of Nationalism or Pan Africanism. Abbee, all over the world, people are trying to unite behind their ethnicity. That is everyone except Black people. We too busy trying to be everything but who we are."

"You know what's amazing about this whole conversation? It was I who was trying to get you to exercise your thinking ability while you were running around in a stupor. Right now Rafique, I'm very proud of you. Alright, now you say all over the world people are uniting behind their ethnicity. What you're missing is the fact that all over the world and for centuries, people have been fighting and killing one another to place one group over another, and when they don't have that, they break it down into tribal groups. The British against the Irish, the Hutus against the Tutsi, Iraqis against Kuwaitis. Nonetheless, why do you think I don't want to see my people united? I don't have to change my Islam for Nationalism. It's perfectly in the realm of Islam for me to identify and have concern for my people. Allah says in the Quran, "I have created you of male and female in tribes and nations so you might identify with one another, but verily the best of you in the sight of Allah is he who is righteous." Yawning, Jamil smiled, stood up and stretched. "Rafique, come give your old man a hug. I truly enjoyed this conversation we had. But right now, I'm so tired, I feel like I'm about to fall out."

Rafique got up and gave his father a warm embrace. "I'm going to my room to make salaat, and then I'm going to bed. I hope you decide through your search for the truth to come back to Islam, but that's a decision you'll have to make on your own, just like I did all those years ago. Whatever you decide though, I'm your father and I'll love you regardless. As salaam alaikum."

"Wa laikum salaam, Abbee. I'm glad we had this talk too."

"Alright son, I'ma see you in the morning." Jamil turned his back and left out of the front room.

Alone now, Rafique yawned before stretching out on the couch. Mentally and emotionally drained from all the days' events, he closed his eyes and in seconds was asleep.

CHAPTER TWELVE

Two weeks later at his home in Philly, Rafique sat in the front room watching television. The smell of tomato sauce and ground beef filled the confines of the apartment as Tracey stood over the stove cooking dinner. The aroma of the food cooking caused Rafique's stomach to growl as he shouted into the kitchen, "Ay, Tracey, what you cooking?"

"Spaghetti!" She shouted back.

Rafique's stomach growled louder and his mouth began to water; spaghetti was his favorite dish. He got up from the couch, picked up the remote and turned the TV off. He was in the mood for some music. As the aroma of the food continued its assault against his sense of smell he sauntered over to the entertainment system, turned the radio on, increased the volume, and returned back to the couch. He exhaled loudly as he flopped back down, closed his eyes, and tried to think of something else besides the food.

Tracey had been planning this day all week. This was little Tim-Tim's weekend at his father's house, making this weekend the perfect time for her girlfriend Buttons and her man to come over for dinner.

Rafique hated these double dates with Tracey's girl-friends and their corny boyfriends. He hadn't met one yet he liked and he especially didn't like Buttons. She was sheisty, always coming at his homie Sean, and all his other homies she had a chance to meet. In his opinion, she was a whore. Every time she came around it seemed as if she had a different boyfriend, like she changed them every sixty days. He didn't like Tracey hanging with her at all, but she was grown and he couldn't choose her friends for her. So as long as Buttons whorish ways didn't rub off on her, he pretty much kept his feelings to himself.

"Rafique," Tracey called out, gently shaking him. Rafique opened his eyes and stared at her.

"Can you turn that down so that we can hear the door-bell? Buttons should be here any minute."

"Go head and turn it down, it's cool. Shit, I was dozing off."

Tracey shook her head, walked over to the entertain-ment system and turned the radio down. No sooner had she turned it down and begun walking back towards the kitchen, the doorbell rang.

"Rafique, can you get that please baby? That's probably her."

"Alright, man," he replied as he slowly stood up, stretched and walked to the front door. The doorbell rang again just as he reached it.

"Who is it?" Rafique called out from behind the closed door.

"It's Buttons, Rafique."

He unlocked the door and opened it to a smiling Buttons.

"Hhheeyyy, Rafique, what's up?"

"What's up, Buttons?"

"Rafique, this my man, Marshon. Marshon, this Rafique."

"What's up, man," Rafique said extending out his hand for a handshake.

"What's up?" Marshon responded, gripping Rafique's hand firmly.

"Come on in y'all. Buttons, lock the door behind you." Rafique said stepping out of the vestibule and leading the way into the front room. "Buttons, Tracey in the kitchen. Give me y'all coats."

As Buttons handed Rafique their coats, she smiled sweetly at Marshon. "Well, I'ma leave you two alone and go help Tracey with the food. You okay, baby?"

"Yeah, I'm cool," Marshon responded.

"Yo man, have a seat, make yourself comfortable," Rafique said as he hung up their coats.

"Thanks, man," Marshon said as he sat on the love seat opposite the couch.

Rafique's immediate impression of Marshon was one of curiosity. He was different from the usual clowns Buttons brought around, who were loud and did a lot of fronting. Marshon was laid back and very quiet. He wasn't like the usual Joe-Joe familiar types that he was used to seeing Buttons with. After a while, the two began to warm up to one another and Rafique began to like him. *Damn, this dude is alright.*

During the course of the evening Rafique learned a lot about Marshon, including the fact that he worked for the post office and he did a little hustling on the side. Upon learning this he automatically began to think of how he could capitalize off this information. Slowly an idea began to take shape in his mind. "Ay, Marshon," Rafique said as the two men sat in the living room listening to Public Enemy while the women cleaned up.

"What's up, man?"

"I just thought about how we can make some money. If you down."

"It depends on what it is."

"Alright, look, I fuck with plastic, you know, credit cards. And I was thinking since you work at the post office, I know you be running into them jawns fresh off the press. All you got to do is run them jawns into me once in a while, and I'll break down half and half."

Marshon didn't respond right away as he thought about Rafique's offer. After a few minutes, though, he began to smile as he nodded in agreement. "Man, I'm with it. I can probably get you like one or two jawns a month."

"Shit, that's good money."

"Marshon, you ready, baby?" Buttons said entering the front room holding their jackets.

"Uh, yeah," Marshon responded, standing up. Rafique stood up as well and shook Marshon's hand.

"Yo, man, it was real good meeting you. When you ready to get with me, get the number from your girl and give me a call.

"Alright, homes, I'ma definitely get with you real soon," Marshon responded while putting on his jacket.

"Alright, Buttons, girl, call me when you get home," Tracey said entering the front room. "It was nice meeting you, Marshon."

"Alright, Tracey." Buttons responded.

"Yeah, it was nice meeting you too. Y'all take care." Marshon said as he and Buttons left out of the apartment.

Rafique locked the door behind them, walked back into the living room and sat next to Tracey on the love seat. "Damn, Tracey, Marshon was alright. He wasn't nothing like the nut ass dudes Buttons usually be with."

"Yeah, he is alright. I hope she don't fuck up with him."

"Tracey, you know your girl is a whore. It's inevitable that she gonna fuck up."

"Rafique, that ain't cool. Why you got to sound my girl like that?"

"Man, I'm just calling it like I see it."

Tracey sucked her teeth, got up and walked into the bedroom.

"Oh, so what you mad now?" Rafique called out after her. Tracey ignored him as she shut the bedroom door.

"Alright, Tracey, I'm sorry." Rafique called out as he got up and followed her to the bedroom.

✷ ✷ ✷

True to his word, Marshon came through once a month. Rafique immediately let Sean know, and by the time winter was at it's mightiest they were rolling in the dough. Par-laying his success, Rafique purchased five pounds of weed, called his young buck C.H. who immediately started selling weed on the strip. Rafique was so absorbed in hustling that he neglected to call Aisha. He hadn't spoken to her in months. She had been calling his mother's home con-stantly, but he could never seem to find the time to call her back. Although his body lay on his soft queen-sized bed in Philly, his mind was in DC with thoughts of Aisha tiptoeing through it. *Damn, I need to call Aisha. I know she probably mad as shit.*

"Rafique!" Tracey calling him from the front room broke up his thoughts.

"Huh?"

"I'm getting read to go to the store. You want something?"

"Naw, baby, I'm cool!"

"Alright, I'ma see you in a little while."

"Alright!"

He waited until he heard the door shut, and immediately picked up the phone, dialed the ten-digit number to DC, turned on the news, and waited patiently for Aisha to pick up.

> "THIS IS LARRY BAIN AND I'M STANDING
> ON THE CORNER OF 49TH AND SPRUCE STREET
> WHERE A BRUTAL MURDER OCCURRED
> EARLIER TODAY…"

Damn, that's right around the way, he thought as he watched the news go into detail about the murder while the phone rang in his ear.

✫ ✫ ✫

"No, Andre," Aisha gasped as Andre licked and sucked on her neck while unzipping her pants. He paid her protest no mind as he slid his hand down her jeans.

"No, this ain't right," she whispered huskily in his ear. "Uuummm," she moaned as his probing fingers located her clit. Like the polar ice caps being melted away by global warming her resistance thawed as she lifted her hips off the bed, and allowed him to remove her jeans.

RING…RING…RING…RING…

As Andre left wet kisses on her inner thighs, Aisha reached over and picked up the phone.

"Hello."

"Eesh, what's up?"

Her stomach knotted up as she shoved Andre to the side and sat up. "Rafique?"

"Yeah, what's up, baby?"

Silence was his answer, as Aisha took a moment before she responded. "Baby? So, what you think, you can just pop in and out my life whenever you want?"

"Yo, I know I ain't been playing my part and I'm sorry."

"No, Rafique, not this time, I'm tired of this shit. You always sorry. I've been waiting around for months and you ain't even have the decency to call me. I can't go through this no more…No stop…"

In a fit of jealousy, Andre snatched the phone, bringing Aisha and Rafique's phone conversation to an abrupt halt.

Rafique became alarmed at hearing the scuffle over the phone. "Hello! Eesh!"

"Yo, what's up?" Andre said into the phone.

"Who the fuck is this?"

"It's Dre."

"Andre?"

"Yeah, Andre."

"Damn man, what the fuck you doing over my girl house?"

"Look, you my man and everything, but this me now."

"Are you serious? Is that what you think? You think you still my man? Naw, nigga, homies don't cross each other like this."

"Fuck you then, nigga, and don't call my woman no fucking more!"

The phone slamming in his ear and a dial tone was the next sound Rafique heard as he held the phone tightly in his hand. He couldn't believe what had just taken place. He always knew that there was a strong possibility that Aisha would find someone else, for he had been neglecting her badly. But not Andre- Andre was supposed to be his man.

Rafique hung up the phone, got out of bed, and stalked to the bathroom. He had to take a shower. He needed to get outside. He was very upset and he needed to cool off some.

Twenty minutes later, with his Timbs strapped up, light blue Guess jeans, dark blue Champion sweat shirt, three quarter black butter leather jacket and wool hat pulled down low over his ears, he was headed out his front door and down to the strip.

Slowly cruising down Chestnut Street, Rafique was still very upset over the phone conversation he just had. With his mind full of images of Andre making love to Aisha, he paid no mind to the sights and sounds that passed by in his peripheral vision as he turned onto 52nd Street. Traffic was thick and slow, and the street lights bright as the neighborhood hustlers, all ready to commence a night's work, took their posts. Strutting back and forth under the spotlights of corner street lamps were all shapes and shades of eye candy, who even on a night as cold as this one were flirting and vying for the attention of the many young hustlers who populated the corners.

Rafique pulled up on 52nd and Delancey Street, parked, got out of the car, and walked towards a crap game that was in full swing. "Come on, Jody, you sticking the dice. Back up some!" Said C.H.

"I ain't moving no fucking where. If you think I'm too close move the wall back. What you gonna do, nigga. My number is six. If you ain't gonna bet, let somebody else fade." Jody responded while shaking the dice.

"Bet a nickel," C.H. responded dropping five one hundred dollar bills on the ground.

"Bet," Jody said as he counted out five hundred and dropped it on the ground.

"I like that six for a tray," Rafique said, coming up on the corner and counting out three hundred.

"Bet that," Manchild said handing Rafique three hundred. Jody waited for everyone to lay down their bets before shooting the dice. With all bets down, the clickity clack of the shaking dice could be heard just above shouts of encouragement and ridicule. Suddenly with the snap of his fingers, Jody shouted, "Number!" as he flung the dice against the wall. In the split second the dice traveled in the air from Jody's open hand to the wall, all conversation ceased, enveloping the crowd in silence. As soon as the dice hit the wall and bounced to the ground, conversation erupted again with everyone collecting their bets.

An hour later, counting a wad of bills, Rafique backed out of the crap game. At that instant Chisel Head Mike pulled up in his money green Acura Legend, blasting Rakim's "Move the Crowd" from his Alpine sound system. Rafique stopped dead in his tracks as the pounding drum beat vibrated throughout his body like a rhythmic heartbeat. His heart rate increased ten fold as it pounded relentlessly against his chest cavity. He looked frantically around him as that strange sense of Déjà vu, instead of slowly invading his consciousness, trampled over him like a stampede of wild horses. *What the fuck, this the same shit that happened in my dream.* He looked to his left and just like he expected he saw his homie Tashi, who like himself had just left the crap game. *Maybe it's a coincidence.* To test this theory, he called out, "Yo, Tash, what time is it?"

"It's, uh, nine thirty."

This shit happening again. It was nine thirty in the dream too.

"Tash, you got some Dumb Dumbs?"

"Yeah, hold up." Rafique watched in amazement as Tashi emptied the sky blue pills out of a small medicine bottle into his open hand. *He's gonna have twenty, just like in my dream.*

"I got twenty. How many you want?"

"Never mind, I'm cool," Rafique responded. Although he was used to events from his dreams becoming reality, it still unsettled him when it happened.

"You cool? Damn, you don't want no Vees! What the fuck is going on? What's up with you?"

"I don't fuck around no more. I don't mess with nothing, not even alcohol."

"Oh yeah?"

"Yeah, that's how I got in that accident. They said I had so much shit in my system that they had to pump my stomach. I almost died from getting high. So, you know, that was enough for me to say that's it."

Rafique was lying so he avoided eye contact as his eyes traced the cracks of the concrete coming to a rest on the tiny blue pills Tashi held in his hand. The real reason why he hadn't touched a drug since leaving the hospital was because of the lesson from his dream. Those tiny blue pills along with codeine cost him a lifetime in the penitentiary. Although it was just a dream it was all too real to ignore, so he made a pledge to himself to never touch another drug. Rafique tore his eyes away from the valiums, the uneasiness he felt beginning to increase. *Fuzz should be coming up shortly.* As this thought ran through his mind, two more of his homes, Buff and Ab walked up on the corner. *It's all coming together. Me, Buff, Tash and Abdul. All that got to happen now is for Fuzz to come up.* He could have left at that point, but he had to see if it would turn out like he knew that it would. So he stood around on that corner for the next hour waiting on Fuzz to show up. Fuzz wouldn't disappoint.

"What's up, y'all?" Fuzz asked, arriving on the corner. Buff, Ab and Tashi spoke back as Rafique just stared at him.

"What's up, Rafique?"

"Ain't nothing up, man." Rafique replied.

Fuzz ignored the cold reply and asked the group, "Any of y'all want to go get some money?" They all declined. If looks could kill, Fuzz would have died a thousand deaths as

Rafique stared hard. *Yeah, motherfucker, I know how this night ends. But it ain't going down like that tonight.*

"Ay, Fuzz, do me a favor?" Rafique asked.

"What's up?"

"Keep my name out your mouth."

"What the fuck you talking about?"

"After tonight, I don't want to hear my name on any shady shit you do. I'm not going nowhere wit you. I ain't trying to get no money wit you, so just don't let me hear my name in anything you connected with."

"Yo, you trippin. What the fuck I'ma say your name for? Everybody here no we don't fuck wit each other like that."

"Whatever, man, you heard what I said."

Instead of responding, Fuzz turned and walked away. Rafique followed him with his eyes. He watched as a black Nissan pulled up across the street and Fuzz headed that way. He watched as a dark skinned guy his size and weight got out the car and shook Fuzz's hand. The two of them stood around and talked for a minute before they both got into the Nissan and pulled off. Turning to Tashi, Buff and Ab, Rafique shook their hands one by one.

"Yo, I'm out," he said. "My fucking head starting to hurt. "Yo, C.H.!"

"Yo," C.H. hollered out from the crap game.

"Come here for a minute. I need to holla at you." C.H. picked up his money and jogged over to where Rafique was standing. "What's up, man?"

"Look, I'm out. Make sure you get with me when you finish up that pound. You still got a lot of weed left?"

"Naw, I'm damn near done. I'ma probably be getting with you in about an hour or two."

"Alright, man."

Rafique's head was still pounding as he turned away, walked to his car, got in, and pulled off. The situation with

Aisha, which caused him to come outside in the first place, had taken a back seat to him trying to figure out a way to avoid what he believed was next – being arrested for a homicide he didn't commit.

CHAPTER THIRTEEN

"**B**itch, get the fuck on the floor and don't move!" shouted Roach as he burst into Sun Rays Drug Store. Dressed in all black, face covered in a mask, he quickly leapt over the counter and went for the cash register.

"Aaaiiiiihhhhh!" the cashier, lying on the cold marble floor with her hands covering her head, screamed hysterically.

"Bitch, shut the fuck up!" Roach stopped struggling to get the register open and kicked the elderly white woman in the ribs, bringing her screams to an abrupt halt.

As all this was going on, Fuzz, also dressed in black with his face covered by a ski mask, entered the drug store right behind Roach and raced to the pharmacy in the back. With a chrome .45 gripped tightly in his hand, he pointed at the stunned pharmacist and shouted threateningly, "Motherfucker freeze, don't move a fucking muscle!" He jumped over the counter, gripped the frightened elderly man by his white lab coat and said, "Do exactly as I say and you won't be hurt. You understand?"

The pharmacist nodded his head as he shook violently with fear.

"Alright, I need for you to show me where the valiums, xanax, and that cough syrup laced with codeine at. Put it all in this bag," Fuzz said, pulling out a plastic shopping bag and he handed it to the pharmacist.

The pharmacist nodded his head again, took the bag and slowly began walking towards the back.

"Bitch, didn't I tell you to shut the fuck up!" With the pain in her ribs throbbing, the cashier laid on the ground crying. Fuzz paid little attention to Roach shouting or the woman crying until he heard three consecutive gun shots.

"What the fuck?!" His heart hammering in his chest, Fuzz swung his .45 and struck the pharmacist in the back of the head, knocking him out cold. He then ran quickly to the front of the store. "Yo, man, come on, we got to go!" he called out to Roach as he headed for the exit.

Roach cussed under his breath and went back to struggling with the register.

"Yo, man, come on! The police will be here any minute!" Fuzz shouted, sticking his head back inside the store. The word 'police' was enough to get Roach moving as he stepped over the cashier's lifeless body, leapt back over the counter and headed for the exit.

☆ ☆ ☆

A pale glow from the floor model television was the only light in the room as Fuzz sat on the worn-down sofa in his grandmother's house. Nervous anticipation was what he felt as sweat beads formed on his forehead. He waited anxiously for the five o'clock news.

Damn, I don't know why I called that crazy motherfucker. He ain't have to shoot that broad. Damn! This nigga got me all caught in a fucking homicide. Stupid motherfucker then killed this white bitch. Damn, calm down, man, we had on masks and gloves. Unless that stupid motherfucker told somebody, we should be cool.

Fuzz picked up the phone, he needed to get his mind off of the murder and his psychotic friend. So he began dialing the one person he could find refuge with, his girl Lisa. *I hope she home, I ain't been able to catch her in a few weeks.* Picking up the phone after a few rings, Lisa interrupted his thoughts.

"Hello."

"What's up, Lisa?"

"What you want?" Lisa responded with an attitude.

"Damn, what's all that about?"

"Look, I ain't got time for all this shit. What you want?"

"Damn, Lisa, did I do something to you or something?"

"Mmaannn, you a nut. Why you keep calling me? Can't you take a hint? I don't call you, you ain't seen me in weeks, and I never take your calls. The only reason why you caught me today was because nobody else is here to answer the phone, so that I can tell them to tell you I ain't home. You see, that's one of your problems, you always thinking it's about you. The way I feel ain't got nothing to do with you, I'm just cool. It's over, so please don't call me no fucking more."

Fuzz was stunned as a click followed by a dial tone rang in his ear. At first he couldn't understand why she was acting like she was. But then, like a light being turned on in a dark room, it came to him. "That bitch probably fucking with somebody else right now. Yeah, that's probably what it is, she probably fucking with that nigga Rafique I seen her all hugged up with." His mind preoccupied with a smoldering jealous rage, he almost missed what he was waiting to see on the news. He turned the volume up, his eyes transfixed on the TV screen as a reporter began:

"THIS IS LARRY BAIN AND I'M STANDING ON THE CORNER OF 49TH AND SPRUCE STREET, WHERE A BRUTAL MURDER OCCURRED EARLIER TODAY.ACCORDING TO POLICE, TWO MASKED, ARMED MEN BURST INTO THIS DRUG STORE DEMANDING DRUGS AND MONEY. WHEN THEY WERE DONE, AN ELDERLY WOMAN LAY DEAD. THE POLICE ARE NOT RELEASING THE VICTIM'S NAME UNTIL HER FAMILY IS NOTIFIED."

So absorbed in the news report, Fuzz didn't notice the phone had rang at least ten times. With his eyes glued to the TV absently, he reached over and answered the phone. "Hello."

"Fuzz, what's up man? This Roach, we on prime time baby. You got the news on?"

"Yeah, yeah, I got it on."

"So, what's up man, we ain't got no money out of that shit. You got something else lined up?"

Fuzz had to be careful. He wanted to tell Roach to stay away from him, but he was scared of Roach. He knew that if he was to say the wrong thing, he would be the next notch on his gun belt. His hand forced, he softly responded, "Let me look into a few things and I'ma get back to you."

"Yo, how long you gonna be? I'm fucked up and I need to get me some paper."

"I'ma call you back in like an hour or so."

"Alright, I'ma holla at you later on."

Fuzz hung up the phone, he felt trapped. He didn't want to deal with Roach anymore, but he was scared to stop. *This that nigga Rafique fault. If he wouldn't have fucked up my thing with Sean, I wouldn't be in this position. Damn, that's it, I'ma get that nigga Sean robbed. I heard he been doing alright. I know he probably got some paper stashed in his house. Yeah, that's*

*it; I'ma put Roach on him. I hope that nigga Rafique there too.
Knowing Roach, he probably gonna pop something, and who better
to get popped than that nigga.*

Satisfied with his next plan of action, he smiled before
stretching out on the coach to take a quick nap.

Fuzz woke up at 9:00, reached over to the coffee table
and picked the phone up. It was time to call Roach back.
The phone rang twice before Roach's deep voice came
through the receiver, "Hello."

"What's up man, this Fuzz?"

"Damn, what's up playboy- you got something for us?".

"Yeah, I know this nigga live out South Philly on this
little back street called Delhi. This nigga just came up on
some serious paper. We can holla at him tonight."

"Oh, yeah, what time?"

"Let me see, its nine o'clock now. Meet me on the strip
at nine thirty."

"Alright, let me throw something on. I'll see you in a
half."

Fuzz hung up the phone, quickly changed his clothes
and headed up the strip. Fifteen minutes later he arrived
on 52nd and Delancey Street where he spotted Rafique,
Buff, Tashi, and Abdul on the corner. *Damn, that nigga ain't
over Sean's house. Even though I don't really fuck with this nigga,
I'ma see if I can get him to ride with us. I know once he see up
pull up on Sean's block he gonna say something. Once he do that I
know Roach gonna get into something with him and that can only
end one way – with Roach popping him.*

"What's up, y'all," Fuzz said once he reached the corner.

Everyone spoke back besides Rafique, who just stared
coldly. Paying Rafique no mind, he asked the group, "Anybody want to go get some money?"

They all declined. Although he was hoping Rafique
would take him up on his offer, he knew that it was a long

shot. But what he wasn't expecting was what Rafique said next. "Ay, Fuzz, do me a favor?"

"What's up?"

"Keep my name out of your mouth."

"What the fuck you talking about?"

"After tonight, I don't want to hear my name in any shady shit you getting ready to do. I'm not going nowhere with you. I ain't trying to get no money with you, so just don't let me hear my name in anything you connected with."

"Yo, you tripping. What the fuck I'ma say your name for? Everybody here know we don't fuck wit each other like that."

"Whatever, man, you heard what I said."

He wanted to respond but instead he just turned and walked away. As he headed across the street, he spotted Roach pulling up in his black Nissan. Fuzz headed in that direction to meet Roach, unaware that Rafique was watching his every move.

CHAPTER FOURTEEN

The nighttime breeze blew gently through the South Philly streets, touching his face like the warm soft caress of a lover. Stars, like brightly colored gems, sparkled against the blackness of space, making the heavens resemble a pirate's lost treasure. Roach took in a deep breath and smiled, revealing a gold cap that covered one of his front teeth and contrasted starkly with his melanin rich skin tone.

He was excited. He always felt this way right before a caper. Stroking the cold steel of a rubber grip, chrome, forty-five automatic, he waited in the piss-stained alleyway that intersected Delhi Street. He had been waiting for the past forty-five minutes for Fuzz to signal him when Sean pulled onto the block. Roach had a clear view of Fuzz, parked diagonally from the alleyway in his black Nissan. They knew that Sean wasn't home because as soon as they got a block away from his house, Fuzz pulled up to the nearest pay phone and called him. The plan after that was for Roach to wait in the alley, and when Fuzz spotted Sean pulling up to the block, he would blink the headlights. Roach would take it from there. So with the patience of a chess master, he waited.

At the fiftieth minute, he saw the headlights blink on and off. *Time to get this paper,* he thought as he waited for Sean to park. Roach stepped out of the alley with his pistol gripped tightly in his right hand, and walked towards the now parked car. He timed his stride perfectly so he reached the car as soon as Sean got out.

"Don't move, motherfucker," he whispered harshly in Sean's ear. Sean froze as he felt the hard hollowed tip of the gun pressed against the back of his head. Sean understood the rules of the game, especially the one on how to act when someone has a gun poking you in the head, so he offered no resistance.

☼ ☼ ☼

Sitting in the dimly lit front room of her house, Ari had just put her baby girl, Diva, to sleep. With her knees pulled up on the couch, she lit up a Newport 100 and took a deep drag. Picking up the remote off the coffee table, she exhaled the pale smoke into the air while flicking through the TV stations. *Damn, ain't shit on TV.* She turned it off and walked over to her stereo system, putting in her Shanice tape. Turning the volume down low, she sat back on the couch and plucked the ashes off her cigarette into the ashtray. *Sean should be back any minute,* she thought while taking another drag from her Newport.

☼ ☼ ☼

"Alright, nigga, this is how it's gonna go down. Let's take a walk to your crib and get that money you got stashed in that motherfucker."

Slowly, Sean began to walk towards his house. *I can't let this motherfucker in my house with my girl and my baby in there. Fuck that.* As he continued on, coming closer and closer to his front door, he tried desperately to come up with an idea on how to avoid taking this man into his home.

Right before he got to his front door, Sean made a decision. *Fuck this.* Disregarding the rules of the game, he spun around with cat like quickness and tried to run away. Caught completely off guard, Roach couldn't believe it when Sean took off. He didn't get very far, though, for the surprise didn't last long. Before Sean got a car length distance away, Roach let off two shots.

The loud clap of two successive gunshots shattered the quiet night and caused Ari to jump with fright. Her heart thundered loudly in her chest as she sat frozen, waiting to hear if more shots were going to be fired. Hesitantly, she got up and walked to the window. The small street was deserted and deathly quiet as she peered up and down the block. Assuming that the worse was over, she quickly walked to her front door and opened it.

Fear fueled his flight as Sean took off, anticipating being struck by bullets. A false sense of confidence came over him when Roach didn't shoot right away. At that instant, the loud retort of the .45 caliber hand gun- followed by hot metal ripping through his back- sent Sean crashing to the cold hard concrete.

Gun in hand, Roach approached his victim, "Stupid motherfucker, don't you know you can't out run bullets."

He kicked Sean's motionless body in the ribs, turned and casually walked back to the car.

Right before he reached the car, an ear-piercing scream burst the still of the night. Roach turned to see a woman running from her house towards the man he left lying critically injured on the sidewalk. Roach smiled and took a step back in that direction. *That's probably that nigga's bitch,* he thought as he began walking back towards Delhi Street.

"Yo, come on, man!" Fuzz called out.

"Hold up, man, that's that nigga's girl. I can get her to take me to that paper."

"Yo, we got to get the fuck out of here. The police will be here any minute."

"Damn, alright man." Roach turned back to the car, got in and shut the door.

✲ ✲ ✲

"Aaaiiiiihhhhh! Oh my God, Sean!" Ari screamed out when she opened the door and saw her man lying face down in a pool of blood. She rushed down the steps to where he lay, crying hysterically. Out of the corner of her eye, she saw Roach take a step back towards her before turning around, getting in a car and pulling off. She filed this away in her mind as she dropped to her knees, rolled Sean on his back and cradled his head in her lap.

"Somebody help me! Help me! Call an ambulance!" she screamed out into the night. "Sean, please don't leave me," with tears streaming down her face, she rocked him back and forth, waiting on help to arrive.

CHAPTER FIFTEEN

Rafique lay flat on his back, a cold rag draped across his forehead. The darkness and silence of his bedroom was a perfect antidote for the throbbing pain of a migraine. Since leaving the strip, his headache had gotten progressively worse, forcing him to get in the bed. He tried to clear his mind of the stress that was brought on by Aisha and then running into Fuzz, but it was to no avail. *This motherfucker probably out there right now killing that dude. I hope I did enough to protect myself. I ain't going back to jail. Damn, listen to me. I ain't going back to jail. You were never in jail. It was just a dream. Plus, who's to say that it's gonna turn out the exact same way. You cool man, everything is gonna be alright. Stop stressing.*

The ringing of the phone interrupted his thoughts and ignited a piercing shot of pain through his temples.

"Aw, shit," he cried out in pain, causing his head to hurt worse.

A shaft of light cutting through the darkness alerted him that Tracey was at the bedroom door. "Rafique, baby, Ari is on the phone. She's hysterical, crying all crazy. I told her that you wasn't feeling too well, but she said it was important. She was saying something happened to Sean."

"Did she say what?"

"No, she just keeps crying. It's almost too hard for me to understand anything she's saying."

"Alright," reaching over the night table Rafique picked up the phone.

"Hello."

"Ra-ra-ra-fique," Ari cried into the phone.

"What's up, Ari? What's wrong?"

"I-t-t-t-'s Sean."

"Ari, calm down. I can hardly understand you. Now what happened to Sean?" Becoming concerned, Rafique sat up in the bed.

Ari took a few seconds to get herself together. She sighed, then words came pouring out. "Somebody shot Sean. They shot him Rafique and I don't know why."

"What! They shot him? Who shot him?"

"I don't know!" She shouted into the phone as the sobs began anew.

"Is he okay?"

"I don't know."

"Where are you?"

"I'm at Jefferson."

"Alright, I'll be right down there."

Rafique hung the phone up and tried to ignore the pain in his head. He wasn't successful as the throbbing continued.

"Is everything okay, baby? What happened to Sean?" Tracey asked, still standing in the doorway.

"Somebody shot him. Get Tim-Tim dressed. We're going down to the hospital. Hand me that bottle of Tylenol on the dresser."

Stepping into the bedroom, Tracey grabbed the pills off the dresser and handed them to Rafique before leaving out to get Tim-Tim dressed.

Opening the bottle, he dumped six of the pills in his hand. He grabbed a glass of water he had sitting next to the phone and took all six, draining the glass as he washed them down.

Twenty-five minutes later, as he drove to the hospital, Rafique's headache had finally subsided, leaving only a dull ache that was more annoying than painful.

"Rafique, where we going?" Tim-Tim asked from the back seat.

"We're going to the hospital."

"Why we going to the hospital?"

"A friend of mine got hurt. You remember Sean don't you?"

"Yeah."

"Well Sean got hurt, so we gonna go check on him."

"Why Sean hurt?"

"Okay, Tim-Tim, that's enough. Question time is over," Tracey interrupted.

As Tracey spoke these words, Rafique was pulling up in the hospital's parking lot. As soon as they entered the building, Rafique spotted Ari. Her normally joyful eyes were red and puffy from crying as she sat sadly in the waiting room.

"Ari!" Rafique called out as he approached.

Ari stood up and walked quickly towards him. Upon reaching him, she embraced him tightly as the tears began to fall again. "They shot my baby," she sobbed.

Gently rubbing her back, he spoke soothingly to her. "It's alright, man, everything's gonna be alright. Have you heard anything from the doctor?"

Sniffling, she responded, "Yeah, he just left. He's in surgery right now.

"Well, how's his chances?" Rafique asked as he relinquished their embrace.

"The doctor says that he'll live, but it may be a while before he walks again."

"He will walk though, right?"

"Yeah, but it just gonna take a minute."

"Ari, right now I need for you to tell me exactly what happened. Hold up, though. Ay, Tracey, go take Tim-Tim to the machine and get him some chips or something, so I can talk to Ari."

Tracey stood directly behind him nodding her head. Before leaving, she spoke to Ari, "Hey, Ari, come give me a hug." As the two women embraced, Tracey spoke softly in her ear, "Whatever you need, don't hesitate to ask. You know, we're here for you. Where's the baby?"

"My mom got her."

"Okay, remember, anything you need." Releasing her embrace, Tracey grabbed Tim-Tim by the hand and led him away.

Alone now, Rafique looked Ari in the eyes and said, "Okay now, tell me exactly what happened."

Tears streamed down her face as she recounted what happened. "I was sitting in the front room listening to the radio, waiting for Sean to come home, when I heard two gun shots. It scared me, but I had a bad feeling, so I got up and walked to the window. I looked outside, but I ain't see nothing. I waited for a few minutes to see if any more gun-shots went off. When it didn't, I walked to the front door and opened it. That's when I saw Sean. Rafique, I never felt a hurt like I did at that moment. Seeing him laying there in a pool of blood, I thought he was dead. It was like a part of me had died too. That's when I screamed and ran to him. I kept hollering, screaming for help as I held his head in my lap. The next thing I know the police and the ambulance was there."

"So you ain't see nobody?"

"No…wait a minute. I did see this guy. He was walking towards a parked car on Fitzwater, but then he turned around and was coming back towards me. But then he stopped and walked back to the car, got in and pulled off."

"Was somebody else in the car?"

"I couldn't see nobody, but it had to be because he got in on the passenger side and the car just pulled off."

"What did he look like?"

"He was dark-skinned, about your size, and he had on this dark sweat suit. It was too dark for me to see exactly what color it was or what his facial features looked like. I just know he was dark-skinned."

"What color was the car?"

"I think it was black. It was a small car, like a Honda or something."

Rafique had to use everything in his power to keep his rage in control. He visibly shook at the effort of maintaining control. *It was Fuzz and that nigga he got in the car with. It got to be him, same dark-skinned dude, and same black car. I know it was that nigga. That's it- I'm getting this motherfucker, him and his homie.*

Rafique kept these thoughts to himself, grabbed Ari's hand and guided her back to the seats where Tracey and Tim-Tim sat waiting.

☆ ☆ ☆

"Man, fuck that!" Roach snapped out, staring at Fuzz coldly.

"What, what's up?"

"You should've let me go back. I could've got that bitch to tell me where that paper at. Now look, nigga, we fucked up. I ain't come all the way up here for nothing. What's up wit them niggas on the Strip?"

"Naw, man, them dudes is alright wit me."

"They alright wit you? How is they alright and they getting all that money up there and you fucked up? Them niggas ain't alright. I'm alright. We, us, we out here in the trenches trying to get this money. Fuck you talking bout, them niggas alright. They getting they shit took tonight, fuck that! Nigga, is you broke?"

"Yeah."

"Alright then, let's go get this money. Broke ass nigga talking about they alright. What, you scared? Nigga, I don't need you to do nothing but keep the car running till I get back, alright?"

"Yeah, man."

"Now cheer up, motherfucker. We getting ready to get paid."

Keeping his eyes on the road as the Nissan zipped through the Philadelphia streets, Fuzz was in a quandary. Although he really didn't care about Roach robbing the Strip, he didn't want to take the chance of being connected to the robbery. He had to live around there. Roach didn't have that problem. He lived all the way in North Philly.

Driving at a moderate speed under the synthetic glow of the city street lamps, the unmistakable click of a round being chambered in Roach's .45 caused Fuzz's anxiety level to rise. Five minutes away from 52nd Street he tried to get Roach to change his mind. "Ay, Roach, how bout if you give me a few minutes to go to my crib to make a few calls so we can get on some real paper."

"Fuzz, do me a favor and shut the fuck up. Stop acting like a bitch. You starting to make me wonder about you. Yo, park on that little block right there."

"On Irving Street?"

"Nigga, I don't know the name of the fucking block. Just park, damn."

Pulling up on 51st and Irving, Fuzz cruised slowly down the block looking for a parking space. Finding one, he pulled over and parked.

"Alright nigga, stay right here. I'll be right back. Oh yeah, not that it matters, but is those niggas strapped?"

"Naw, the police be rolling up too much for them niggas to be standing around with guns. They be having them jawns stashed in the alley.

Nodding his head, Roach opened the car door and stepped out into the night. Tucking his gun in the waistline of his sweat pants, Roach strolled confidently towards 52nd Street.

By the time Roach reached 52nd and Delancey Street, most of the hustlers had gone. It was Friday night and the Dynasty, a neighborhood club, was jumping. With promises of one-night stands, alcohol, and dancing, only a couple of the hungriest and most dedicated hustlers remained. Hawking their illegal products and watching the crap game, they were unaware of the threat that rapidly approached. Although not as crowded as it was earlier, the crap game still held a few die hard gamblers, each one focused on the game and oblivious to everything else.

Roach smiled as the situation on the corner became clear. *This shit sweet, it's gonna be easier than I thought. Look at these stupid motherfuckers. They ain't even paying attention and it ain't a strap out here either.* As this thought flashed through his mind, he arrived at the crap game. Wasting no time, he moved into action. "Get the fuck up against the wall! Leave that fucking money on the ground! You niggas know what it is, don't make it no worse!" Brandishing his .45, he watched them closely as they scrambled to put their hands on the wall. Satisfied at their compliance, he barked out more orders. "Yo, you with that Phillies cap on, come here."

His heart pounding in fear, the young man slowly removed his hands from the wall, turned and faced Roach.

"Here, take this bag." Pulling out a plastic shopping bag from his pocket, he tossed it to the petrified young man. Catching it out the air, the young man held it and stared at Roach.

"Alright, empty your pockets and put the contents in the bag. Then I need you to pick up all the money off the ground and put that in the bag. Then take all these niggas jewelry and turn their pockets inside out, check their socks and put everything you find in the bag, toss it back to me and then get the fuck back against the wall. And hurry the fuck up. This shit I'm doing ain't legal!"

Moving quickly, the young man did as he was told. Taking all the jewelry, emptying everyone's pockets, checking socks and picking up the money off the ground, in less than five minutes he was tossing the bag back to Roach and was getting back against the wall.

"I'm walking off the block right now. If I see one of you nut ass niggas turn around, all y'all gonna get it." With that, Roach backed up off the block. As he reached the corner, he turned and sprinted the two blocks to Irving Street where Fuzz waited with the car running. Hopping in the car, he threw the bag to the back seat and said, "Let's ride. That shit was sweet. All them niggas had some paper on em, and I got the crap game and some jewelry."

Fuzz nodded his head, pulled off and headed for home. They had to go split the loot up. Twenty minutes later, Roach was leaving out of Fuzz's house. "Ay, Fuzz, if any of this shit comes back on you, just call me and I'll take care of it."

Fuzz knew that Roach meant every word he said. With that reassurance, he felt a lot better. "Alright, Roach, I'ma holla at you later."

"Alright, Fuzz," Roach smiled, his gold tooth sparkled as he turned and stepped out into the Philadelphia night.

CHAPTER SIXTEEN

With the silence of a city asleep and the lonely whistle of a cold January wind for company, Rafique sat in his car lurking beneath the dark shadows of a walnut tree. 54th and Delancey Street resembled the streets of an old western ghost town, as most people were in their homes sleeping. This is what most people did at three-thirty in the morning, but not Rafique. He was on a mission.

Like a brand new wound bleeding profusely, his anger at what happened to Sean was still fresh. It flowed through his veins contaminating his mind, simmering just below the surface as it sought an avenue of escape, but he was able to hold it in check. This was why he sat in the shadows. He was determined to make those he thought responsible for the bullet in his homies back pay for what they did.

The wind howled angrily and tree limbs groaned in protest as a gust hurtled down the street pushing an empty beer can. It rattled loudly as it rolled down the street, corrupting the still night. Rafique paid little attention to the sounds of the cold ghetto night, for his focus was keen. One thing was on his mind and one thing only: Fuzz. Fuzz, and whoever else he led him to, was going to pay, and pay dearly.

Although he sat patiently, an immeasurable amount of hatred brewed in Rafique's soul and provided the energy to keep him focused during the long wait. Slowly, the minutes ticked by, but he was unfazed by time. With images of Fuzz testifying against him on the witness stand keeping him occupied, time was not an issue. These images fueled that raging fire of hate that consumed everything, even his recognition of time.

His black leather driving gloves, with the knuckles protruding, gripped the steering wheel tight. The hard metal of his black 9 mm felt heavy as it rested on his lap. Removing one of his hands from the steering wheel, without thought, he traced the outline of the gun. At that moment he saw Fuzz through the rearview mirror rounding the corner. *Here that motherfucker go right now*, he thought as images of Sean being shot in the back flashed through his mind. Grabbing his gun with one hand and opening the car door with the other, he got out, and, like a black angel of death, emerged from the shadows.

"Yo, Fuzz, what's up man?" Rafique called out calmly trying to keep Fuzz at ease so he could get close to him.

"Yo, who that?" Fuzz answered squinting his eyes.

"It's Rafique."

Fuzz slowed his gait as thoughts of what happened to Sean ran through his mind. *Damn, do this nigga know? He can't know, ain't nobody see me.* Though his heart raced with fear, he continued to walk towards Rafique.

This motherfucker ready to run, Rafique thought as he noticed Fuzz slowing down. Hiding his pistol behind his thigh, the hatred and the need for revenge struggled to break loose as he fought with himself to maintain control. He needed to get closer, he couldn't afford to spook him.

"Yo, what you doing around here this time of night?" Fuzz asked camouflaging his fear.

"I need to holla at you," Rafique responded, maintaining his calm demeanor as he got within range.

"Holla at me about what?"

Slowly Rafique brought his gun from behind his leg, all pretenses of calmness gone. "I need to know why the fuck you had my man shot and who was that nigga you had with you tonight?" With the gun trained on Fuzz's forehead, it took every ounce of control for Rafique not to pull the trigger.

"Wh-wh-wh-what you talking about Fique? What you mean Sean got shot? What nigga?"

"Oh, you want to play games, huh?" Advancing quickly, Rafique erased the few feet that separated them and brought the gun crashing down atop Fuzz's head.

"Aaaaahhhh!" Fuzz hollered out as he crumbled to the ground. Blood gushed from a gash on the top of his head as he frantically tried to stop the bleeding with his hands. Dazed, Fuzz looked up at Rafique, his eyes pleading. "Come on, man, why you doing this?"

"Shut the fuck up! Now, I'ma ask you one more time, who the fuck was with you?" Rafique chambered a round in his gun and pressed it against Fuzz's head.

Feeling death near, Fuzz broke, "Yo, man, don't do this. I'll tell you who it was."

Confirmation!

Although he was almost one hundred percent certain Fuzz was behind Sean getting shot, hearing him practically admit it almost caused him to squeeze the trigger. *Not yet, I still need him*, he reminded himself. "Who the fuck was it then?"

"It was Roach, man! He wasn't supposed to shoot him, we was only gonna rob him. Fique, man, I ain't even get out the car. Sean was alright with me. That nigga wasn't supposed to shoot him. I ain't have nothing to do with him getting shot."

His hands shaking with rage, Rafique looked at Fuzz incredulously. *Either this nigga think I'm a nut or he's out of his fucking mind.* Staying in control, he spoke softly, "I need for you to get him down here."

"When, now?"

"Yeah, now."

"How I'ma do that? It's like four in the morning."

"You know what, you right, I tell you what, we just gonna get it done tomorrow night. You gonna have to sleep in the trunk."

"What? The trunk? Come on Fique, man, look I promise you I'ma get the nigga to come down, just get with me later on."

"Shut the fuck up and stand up!" Digging in his coat pocket, Rafique pulled out a pair of handcuffs. "Here, cuff yourself," he said throwing the cuffs to Fuzz.

"Cuff myself? Yo man, you ain't go—,"

"Motherfucker!" was all Rafique said as he swung his pistol again striking Fuzz and opening a gash just above his right eye. Fuzz tumbled back to the ground, and blood immediately began to pour down his face. Dazed and bloody, Fuzz began to plead for his life.

"Please, man, you don't have to do this. I'll do whatever you need me to do."

Rafique was silent for a moment as his blood shot eyes bore a hole through his soul. Without warning, he drew back his size nine Timberland boot and kicked Fuzz in the ribs with all his might.

"Uuuugghh." Fuzz groaned as all the air escaped his lungs.

"Pick them fucking cuffs up and put them on."

Crawling, blood dripping from his gashes, Fuzz fumbled around looking for the cuffs. Fuzz found the cuffs and rose to his knees. With his hands shaking as if he was suffering from Parkinson's disease, he struggled to cuff himself. After a few seconds he could hear the tell-tale click, his hands were secured.

Rafique leaned over, grabbed the taller man by his coat and forcefully yanked him to his feet. "Alright, nigga, move."

With Rafique's gun sticking him in the back, Fuzz slowly walked across the street praying that someone would spot him. But on this night, his prayers would go unanswered. They reached the shadow of the walnut tree and Rafique's car, where they stopped.

"Right here, lean against the car and don't move. If you try to run, I'ma chase you down and blow your fucking brains out."

Totally defeated, Fuzz slowly slumped against the car as blood continued to flow from his wounds. Rafique opened the trunk and looked at Fuzz coldly. He motioned with his head, "Alright, nigga, get the fuck in."

Fuzz complied without an argument. He figured if he did what Rafique said, maybe he just might get out of this alive. Lying on his side, he looked up at Rafique searching for signs of mercy. He didn't see any, though, as Rafique slammed the trunk on his hope and left him in total darkness.

Rafique got in the car, put the key in the ignition, and pulled off. He obeyed all the traffic laws as he headed for Center City and one of the all-night parking garages where his homie Vern worked the graveyard shift. It took him fifteen minutes traveling down the deserted morning streets to arrive at the garage. He stopped at the booth to get his ticket.

"Yo, what's up, Fique? What you doing down here so early?"

"What's up, Vern? Man, me and my woman been arguing all night. I just had to get the fuck out the house. I ain't been to sleep yet, so I figured I'd come down here and just sleep in my car."

"Yo, you crazy man," Vern said handing Rafique the ticket he would need to leave the garage. "Yo, I'm out at six."

"Alright then, Vern. I'ma probably be asleep by then. Call me later on."

"Alright, Fique."

Rafique pulled into the garage, and drove to the second level, found a spot in the far corner and parked. He turned the car off, reclined his seat back and closed his eyes. *Damn, what the fuck am I doing?* For the first time since he found out Sean had been shot, Rafique began to think clearly.

Without anger clouding his mind, he began to see the possible consequences of his actions. Like a motion picture, his dream began to play in his mind – the ass crack searches, the walls of the pen, and all the pain that he caused his family when he received a life sentence. It all caused second thoughts to creep into his mind. *I should just scare this motherfucker real bad and then let him go. Yo, you tripping man. Get your shit together. You letting this dream shit bug you the fuck out. Scare him and let him go, huh? Then what? You think he gonna let this shit ride? What about his man? You don't even know what he look like. So what you gonna do, go through life looking over your shoulder on some paranoid shit, wondering every time a dude walk up on you is he gonna kill you?*

At this point, Rafique knew he had to go all the way. It was too late to turn back now. It was either live a life of paranoia, always looking over his shoulder, or eliminate the problem completely. Resigned to this fact, exhaustion overcame him as he fell into a troubled sleep.

✻ ✻ ✻

A cool chill seeping through the fog of sleep caused Rafique to reach over and pull the covers back over him. *Tracey always hogging the covers,* he thought as the covers immediately knocked off the chill. As sleep began to re-stake its claim over him, he was startled awake by his front door crashing in, and sounds of feet running towards the bedroom. As he awakened, Tracey grabbed him tight and shouted, "Rafique, what's happening?!" He didn't have time to answer as laser points dotted their bodies and shouts of, "Police! Get on the floor!" rang out in the bedroom.

Ten minutes later, as he was handcuffed and being led out into the cold morning with nothing on but his box-ers, Rafique turned to the nearest detective and asked, "Yo, what the fuck is going on?"

"We have a warrant for your arrest."

"For what?"

"Homicide."

"Homicide?"

"Yeah, apparently somebody saw you put that guy in the trunk."

Rafique didn't respond as he stepped into the open doors of the paddy wagon. He took one last look at his home and his woman crying hysterically on their porch as a lone tear traveled the length of his face and the wagon doors slammed shut.

✻ ✻ ✻

Rafique jumped up out of his sleep, his heart pounding in his chest. He looked around, confused at first. *Damn, I was just dreaming.* Slowly, his surroundings and situation became clear. He checked his watch, put his key in the ignition, and started the car up. It was time to finish this.

✵ ✵ ✵

"No, Steve, you ain't gonna lie your way out of this one. You was supposed to take me out last night. Not only didn't you show up, you ain't even call me." Roach's girl, Nicky, said with a pout.

Roach flashed his trademark gold tooth smile and looked his girl in the eye. "I know I was out of pocket. But on some real shit, something came up that I had to take care of." Roach reached in his pocket and pulled out a roll of money. "I got to get that paper, Nicky. Or would you rather I was a broke ass nigga?"

Nicky's eyes lit up at seeing the money. "Give me some money, Steve, and I'll see about forgiving your ass for standing me up."

Roach laughed as he peeled off a couple hundred dollars and gave it to her.

"Thank you, baby," Nicky said as she put the money in her Coach bag. "Is you gonna spend some time with me today?" she asked, her voice dripping with sex. She got up, her eyes filled with lust and straddled his lap. She moaned as she placed a wet kiss on his mouth. Hungrily, he responded as his hands began squeezing her soft round ass.

"Uuummm," she moaned as his kisses moved from her mouth to her neck. Trapped in this moment of pleasure, he paid no mind to the phone as it began to ring.

"Steve!" his mother called down into the basement.

"Huh?" Roach shouted back as Nicky continued kissing him, moving to his neck.

"Somebody wants you on the phone!"

"Alright, mom! Nicky, hand me that phone." Clearly agitated at being interrupted, Nicky sucked her teeth before picking up the phone and handing it to him.

"Hello."

"Roach, what's up, man. This Fuzz."

"Yo, what's up, man. I'm kind of busy right now." Roach said as Nicky reached down while sucking his neck to massage his dick.

"Yo, man, these niggas is on my top. They saying I set 'em up. One of them crack me upside the head with a gun and split my shit open."

"What?! Hold up, Nick, move." Rolling her eyes, Nicky moved. "Alright, now, what happened?"

"This afternoon I was going to the store and like five niggas stepped to me. They was trying to get me to tell them who you was. I barely got away."

"Alright, you know where they live?"

"Yeah."

"Alright, I'm on my way."

Roach hung up the phone and looked at Nicky, who was clearly upset. "Nick, I got to go."

"Yeah, yeah, I know. How long you gonna be?"

"I don't know but it shouldn't take too long. You gonna wait for me here?"

"Should I?"

"Yeah, you better."

"Alright, I'ma stay. Steve…"

"Huh?" Roach responded as he stood up.

"Baby, be careful out there."

"Always," he said, flashing his gold tooth grin.

✵ ✵ ✵

A blistering wind sweeping through the narrow streets was bone-chillingly cold as Rafique stood on the corner watching Fuzz talk to Roach on the phone. Although Rafique was dressed warmly, his extremities were beginning to feel the wind cut through his clothing. In a futile effort to warm them up, he began throwing punches. Finally, Fuzz hung up the phone.

"Alright, man, I did what you said, he on his way. Can you please let me go now?"

"Not yet. I need for you to stick around just in case your man don't show up."

"Fique, man, I'm telling you he gonna show up. He on his way now."

"Alright then, you ain't got nothing to worry about. Here put these cuffs back on, you got to get back in the trunk."

Still clinging to the hope that Rafique would let him go, Fuzz didn't complain as he put the cuffs back on and walked obediently to the car.

Once Fuzz was tucked securely in the trunk, Rafique sat in his car across the street from Fuzz's home and waited on Roach. Twenty-five minutes later, he spotted the black Nissan slowly turn the corner and pull onto Delancey Street. Rafique quickly got out of the car as Roach drove by. As luck would have it, there was a parking space directly in front of Fuzz's front door. Rafique picked up his pace and tried not to seem in a hurry. He timed his stride perfectly, reaching Roach's car just as he was opening the door. With one fluid motion, he reached for his waistline, drew his gun, and let off four shots. Two found their mark, hitting Roach in the chest. The other two struck the car seat. His eyes wide with shock, Roach fell face first out of the car, his body bent at an awkward angle. Without any time to waste,

Rafique walked up on him and let loose two more shots, hitting Roach in the head.

"Punk motherfucker, that's for Sean." He kicked Roach's lifeless body in the ribs, quickly turned, jogged to his car, got in and calmly pushed off.

✳ ✳ ✳

The loud clap of four successive gunshots made Fuzz jump with fright and caused him to hit his head on the roof of the trunk. Pain shot through his head as he cried out in agony, he had reopened one of the gashes on his head. Warm blood flowed down the side of his face, touching the corner of his mouth and filling it with the taste of his life fluid. *I hope Roach got that motherfucker,* he thought as he tried to shift positions in the cramped up space he occupied. Two more shots exploding caused his heart rate to accelerate with fear and anxiety. Seconds later, the car door opening and closing dashed all hopes of Roach being alive. With his life hanging in the balance, Fuzz began to doubt that Rafique would let him go. *I'm a witness, he ain't gonna let me go,* he thought as the car started up and began to move. *If he was gonna let me go, why not in front of my house? Come on, Fuzz, man, he just shot a nigga he ain't got time to let you out the fucking trunk.* Fuzz clung to the possibility that Rafique would let him live and he tried to remain optimistic. *Where the fuck he taking me?* This question would go unanswered as tears began leaking down his cheeks in the darkness, and all hope of being allowed to live began to fade away.

He couldn't tell how long they had been driving when the car came to a stop. It could have been two hours or ten minutes. His sense of time had been ruined by fear and all the time he had spent crammed in the trunk. He felt the car come to a stop, and, hearing the door open, his anxiety levels increased. The time it took for Rafique to get out of the car and open the trunk seemed to move in slow motion.

"Goddamn, man, what you shit on yourself or something?" Rafique asked as the trunk door opened and the smell of being locked in a small space, bloodied and without ventilation, escaped the confines of the trunk and assaulted Rafique's nose. "Look, you gonna have to walk home. Come on, get out."

He gonna let me live. Relief washed over Fuzz as a huge smile crept across his face. Rafique grabbed Fuzz by the arm and helped him out the trunk.

Nothing but trees surrounded them as Fuzz checked out the area. "Yo, man, where we at?"

"Where we at? We at the last place you gonna see alive. That's where the fuck we at."

"Yo, Fique, come on ma—"

The loud roar of Rafique's 9 mm discharging shattered the silence of the park and left Fuzz's last sentence unfinished. Fuzz was frozen in shock as the bullet left a hole the size of a nickel in the middle of his forehead. The hot metal of the bullet slammed into his skull and shattered, sending metal shards into the soft flesh of his brain, ripping it apart. He died instantly.

CHAPTER SEVENTEEN

On his way home from Fairmount Park, Rafique drove slowly through the night time streets. With the radio turned off, the only sounds that could be heard were the occasional passing cars and the loud thump of his car's shock absorbers, absorbing the impact of driving over pot holes. Sweat glistened on his face and forehead and flowed steadily down the sides of his cheeks. Although air flowed continuously through the heating vents keeping the car warm, it wasn't the heat that had him sweating.

Like a cancer, paranoia had infiltrated his being, malignant tumors of extreme wariness multiplying, infecting his body and his mind, causing him to think irrationally. *Fuck! What if somebody saw me shoot that nigga on the block? What if somebody saw me put Fuzz in the trunk? Fuck this, I'ma just leave town for a few weeks, and let shit cool down for a minute. I can tell C.H. to keep his ears open and let me know if my name comes up.* His heart hammered in his chest as the grip of paranoia became tighter. *I'm getting the fuck out of here tonight.* Nervously he checked his rearview mirror for the police before wiping the sweat off his brow and turning on the radio.

✷ ✷ ✷

Tracey sat in the front room of their apartment, her face riddled with worry. She hadn't seen or heard from Rafique since they had left the hospital two days ago. She stared absently at the television, her mind wandering back to the last time she saw him.

They had pulled up to the curb in front of their home but instead of turning the car off, Rafique just sat there with the engine running.

"Ain't you gonna park?" Tracey asked, staring at him perplexed.

His eyes locked in front of him, and his voice devoid of any emotion, he responded, "Naw, I got to take care of something."

Tracey sighed and ran her fingers through his hair before responding. "Rafique, I know you're upset about Sean, but baby please think about this first. Don't go out there and do something you'll live to regret. Remember what happened in that dream, baby. Please, Rafique, just come inside and cool off some."

"Tracey, get out. I'll be home later," he said, ignoring her pleas.

Tears streamed down her face as she refused to move. Slowly, Rafique turned to look at her. He reached over and wiped the tears from her eyes. He felt that he needed to reassure her, so he learned over and kissed her on the cheek, "Look, I ain't gonna do nothing dumb. I just need some time to myself, that's all. I'll be home a little later on, alright?"

Although she knew he was lying, she nodded her head slowly, opened the car door, and got out. Rafique pulled off as soon as she closed the door. She watched as the tail lights grew smaller and smaller until they were no longer in sight. As the tears continued to fall, she dropped her head and walked quickly to the house.

The lock to the front door clicking jolted her out of her memories. *He's home.* An overwhelming sense of relief flooded her being, washing away the worry, as she got up to meet her man.

"Rafique, baby, I was so worried about you. Where have you been?" Tracey asked as Rafique stepped out of the vestibule and into the front room.

Still in the grip of paranoia, Rafique didn't answer right away. Instead he walked to the window, pulled the curtain to the side and peered out into the night.

"What's wrong, baby? Tracey asked. "Who's outside?"

Satisfied that he wasn't being followed, he closed the curtains and began walking to the bedroom. "Look, I ain't got a whole lot of time."

Her heart racing, Tracey followed closed behind him. "What, Rafique? What's wrong?"

"I got into a little situation and I got to leave town for a minute," he responded entering the bedroom.

Tracey stood stunned watching as he pulled out a Nike duffle bag and began packing clothes. "Leave town? Why Rafique?"

"Look, all that ain't necessary to know. Im'a need for you to give C.H. weed whenever he runs out. I already got it bagged up. It's separated into pounds. You know where it's at right?"

Slowly, she nodded her head.

"All you got to do is collect the money and give him the weed. He probably gonna be dropping some money off soon. When you get it you can use whatever you need. So, you know, you should be cool while I'm gone."

"I should be cool? How Rafique? How Im'a be cool? Rafique, you scaring me."

His duffle bag stuffed, Rafique zipped it up and faced his woman. He watched the tears stream down her face, and, like a hard slap, a lesson conveyed to him through his dream finally hit home. How he lived his life, and the negative consequences from actions without thought, not only affected him, but it affected the people that cared for him as well.

He approached her slowly and gripped her in a strong embrace. He could feel the rapid beat of her heart with her soft body pressed tightly against his. He stroked her hair and whispered softly in her ear, "Tracey, don't worry. Everything's gonna be alright. I just got to go for a few weeks, that's all. As soon as I straighten this shit out, I'll be back. I promise you, man, everything gonna be okay.

"Are you sure?" She asked, choking back the sobs.

"Yeah, I'm sure. Look as soon as I get to where I'm going, I'ma call you, okay?"

She stepped back and looked into his eyes, "Where are you going? When are you leaving?"

"I'ma go out D.C. If you need to contact me, just call my pop. I was gonna leave tonight, but I can't leave you here feeling all fucked up so I'ma leave tomorrow okay." He pulled her close again and kissed her on the forehead before moving to the mouth, where all the passion and love that they felt for one another was expressed with the dance of their tongues.

CHAPTER EIGHTEEN

Steam filled the bathroom as Monique stepped out of the shower, dripping wet. She grabbed the towel from off a hook and dried off before opening up the bathroom to release the fog. She wiped the condensation off the clouded mirror so she could look at her reflection. She smiled, displaying a deep set of dimples and her pearly whites. She admired the image that smiled back. Pulling off her shower cap, she left the bathroom and walked naked to her bedroom. She stopped at the full-length mirror that adorned her closet door and stared at her reflection again, vainly taking in the pleasure she received from looking at the voluptuous curves of her body. The phone ringing interrupted her self-admiration. Annoyed at the interruption, she left the mirror, walked over to her nightstand where the phone rested, and picked up.

"Hello."

"Monique, what's up girl? You miss me?"

"Rafique?"

"Of course, who else could it be?"

"I was just making sure, and yeah I miss you." She responded, taking a seat on the bed. "Where you at?"

"I'm in Philly but I'm on way back out there, you busy?"

"No, I just got out the shower. I was just getting ready to watch a little TV before I got in the bed."

"Well, you think you can wait up for me?"

"Yeah."

"Well, alright, I should be out there by nine. What's the address? I remember you live on Division Avenue but all them houses look the same on that block."

She laughed as she gave him the address. They talked for a few minutes longer before hanging up. She got up, slipped on a red lace panty and bra set and sprayed a little Chanel No. 5 on all her special places before squeezing into some extra tight short-shorts and putting on an over-sized tee-shirt. Strutting back to the full length mirror, she pulled her hair back into a pony-tail, held it together with a rubber band, and took another self-admiring look in the mirror before leaving the bedroom and walking downstairs to the front room.

At the bottom of the stairs, she felt along the wall for the light switch. She found it, clicked it on and flooded the room in light. Her steps were light as she seemingly floated across the room to her stereo system. She pushed the power button on the radio and tuned the station to WPGC and the Quiet Storm. As the soft melodies of old school and contemporary R & B hits flowed through the two three-foot tall speakers, she took a seat on the couch, closed her eyes, and began thinking about Rafique and the first time she laid eyes on him.

She had been bored to death at her job as a sales clerk at Urban Wear. Constantly checking her watch, it seemed as if time were moving in slow motion as she waited impatiently for her shift to end. *Two more hours,* she thought. It was at that exact moment when he walked through the entrance. She could see that he was with a girl but that didn't stop her from staring. He was perfect. Everything that she was attracted to in a man physically, he had. From his complexion to the shape of his eyes, to his style of dress, to his slim build. And he was bow legged. She had to meet him, but he was with someone else. A slight pang of jealousy shot through her body as she turned her back to him, resigned to the fact that she probably would never get a chance to meet him.

She felt the stare before she actually turned around and saw him looking. *Damn, he got a lot of heart staring at me like that right in front of his woman.* Boldly, she stared back, watching as he said a few words to his girl before she walked away to look at some clothes. He then headed straight for her. Her heart raced as he held her gaze and steadily approached. He came to a stop in front of the counter, stood and stared. Not wanting to show that she was attracted to him, she spoke out as if she had an attitude. "Um, excuse me, can I help you?

"Oh damn, my fault, but is your name Monique?"

How do he know my name? she thought before asking him.

"How do you know my name?"

"You probably don't remember me but I was in your first grade class."

That's game, he probably just know somebody that know me and they told him my name. She went along with it anyway.

"Yeah, you right. I don't remember you. But how you remember me from all those years ago?"

"You never forget your first love. I use to have a serious crush on you. But back then I was scared of girls. I was real shy."

She smiled, "Are you still scared of girls? Do you still have a crush on me?" *Uhm, he got a sexy ass smile.*

Rafique returned her smile with one of his own. "To your first question, naw I ain't scared of girls no more, and to your second question, believe it or not, yeah."

"Well, that's a good thing."

"Is it?"

"Yeah."

"Damn, let me apologize, I ain't even introduce myself. Since you don't remember me, my name is Rafique."

"Rafique, huh? Well, Rafique, where you from cause I can tell by the way you talk you ain't from around here."

"Yeah, I'm from Philly. I got family out here, though."

"How long you in town for?"

"I'm only here til Sunday."

She watched him closely as his eyes traveled upward to something behind her. *He probably looking in the mirror at that bitch trying to creep up behind him.* Monique smiled and shook her head. She was right and what he said next confirmed her thoughts.

"Listen, Monique, I'm here with my friend so I can't holla at you right now. Are you going to be here tomorrow?"

"Yeah."

"What time you get off?"

"Tomorrow I get off at six."

"Alright, I'ma stop by then to pick you up so we can talk some more. As a matter of fact, we're going out to eat. But look, I got a proposition for you."

"What's up?"

"I got a credit card I just found and I want to use it. If you down, I'll give you a hundred to let me use it here."

"Shit, I don't care. Ain't none of this shit mine."

After he paid her, and he and his girl used the credit card to it's max, they left. But that wasn't the last time she saw him. He came back the very next day, picked her up from work, and took her out to eat. During their meal, they got to know one another a little better. She found out that he was easy to talk to, intelligent, he made her laugh and he had a little money, which was always a good thing. After a while she began to feel very comfortable around him, so much so that it was as if she had known him all her life. She found herself telling him everything about her. How she was single, living alone in a house that her parents left her after they died in a car accident. She told him about her ex-lovers, what she liked and disliked, and what her plans for the future were. He had an uncanny ability to extract information without giving any in return, but at the same time creating a feeling in you as if you knew all there was to know about him. But as she thought it over, she still knew very little about him. He was still pretty much a mystery to her.

After they finished eating, he drove her home where they ended the night standing on her porch and sharing a very intimate kiss. Armed with each other's numbers when he left and went back to Philly, they were able to stay in contact with one another, slowly laying the foundation to what they both wanted- a relationship.

Now, a couple of months later, she would finally be seeing him again and she was nervous with anticipation. She got up off the couch and walked back up the stairs to her bedroom where she began lighting scented candles. Already placed strategically around the room for maximum romantic effect, she turned out the lights and watched as the shadows of the flames danced on the walls. Satisfied with the candle light, she walked over to her dresser where her radio and cassette player sat. She reached over, picked up her Keith Sweat tape and inserted it into the tape deck. She turned the volume up, smiled and nodded her head in approval. Monique wanted the mood to be just right when he arrived. If left up to her, after tonight, Rafique would never go back to Philly.

✻ ✻ ✻

Rafique stepped out of the warm confines of his car, and tucked his exposed chin trying to protect it from the biting wind. You would think that with the temperature in the single digits, sane people would be indoors hiding from old man winter's bite, and they were. But on the strip, the drive to escape poverty, the influence of rampant materialism, and an insatiable urge to catch that elusive dream of cocaine bliss, drove the sane to do some insane things.

This was why on a night as cold as this one, a few young hustlers and hope-to-die drug addicts braved the elements in a never-ending game of serve and consumption of black misery. Rafique's pace was brisk as he approached 52nd & Delancey Street, one of the corners where this game was being played out, and walked up to C.H.

"Yo, C.H.!"

C.H. turned in the direction he heard his name being called. He spotted Rafique approaching and walked to meet him. "What's up, Fique," he said removing his glove and exposing his hand to the frigid temperatures in order to shake Rafique's hand.

Rafique removed his glove in kind, gripped C.H.'s hand and shook it as he responded, "What's up, C.H.?"

"It's cold as a motherfucker out here, but I got to get this paper, that's what's up." A cloud of vapor escaped his mouth as he spoke, but just as soon as it appeared the wind quickly snatched it away.

"Yo, man, I'm about to leave town. You got some money on you?" Rafique asked.

"Yeah, I got about fifteen hundred on me."

"Alright, let me get that."

C.H. reached in his pocket, pulled out the money and gave it to him. "How long you gonna be gone?"

"I don't know. I might be gone for a month maybe more. Ay, Cee man, this don't mean go on no fucking syrup drinking binge again."

"I know, I know. I'm cool, man. I don't fuck around no more. The only reason why I went out like that last time was because I thought you was dead. I was in mourning. But now I'm trying to get rich and I know getting high and getting rich is like two dicks with no bitch. It don't mix."

Rafique laughed, "You always got some fly shit to say. Alright, Cee man, I'm trusting you to get this money. Look, everything still gonna be popping. Tracey gonna take care of you while I'm gone. Oh, yeah, one more thing, I'ma need you to do something."

"What's that?"

"Put your ear to the ground and let Tracey know if my name comes up in anything."

"Anything like what?"

"Whatever, anything, if my name come up just let her know."

"Alright, man. Oh yeah, Fique."

"What's up?"

"You heard about the nigga that got killed on 54th and Delancey last night?"

"Naw, who was it?"

"I ain't hear who it was. I just know somebody got the shit shot out of em."

"Naw, man, I ain't hear nothing about it."

"Alright then, man, let me get back to this paper."

"Alright, Cee, I'm out man. Im'a see you when I get back."

With that said, Rafique shook C.H.'s hand once again, turned around and headed back to his car. His heart thundered in his chest because of the murder C.H. mentioned.

Paranoia once again invaded his conscious causing overly suspicious thoughts to run wild in his mind. *I wonder if I drew on myself? C.H. might have figured out I had something to do with that shit, especially since I asked him to let Tracey know if my name came up in anything. Damn, I'm tripping. C.H. ain't notice shit. Relax, nigga.* Taking a deep breath, Rafique calmed himself down as he continued on to his car.

Before he reached the shelter of his Jetta, he had to endure a few more minutes of the cold as he stopped at the corner pay phone. Rafique smirked as he recalled his stolen calling card number and dialed the ten-digit number to D.C. At that instant he decided that Monique's house would be his first stop upon reaching the Chocolate City.

The artificial glow of the highway lights fought the blackness of night to a standstill, illuminating what would otherwise be a highway shrouded in total blackness. The traffic on I-95 was virtually non-existent as Rafique cruised at a moderate speed of sixty-five miles per hour. Soft music played softly just above a whisper, but he paid the music no mind. Deep inside of him, two souls fought to possess him solely and totally.

As he traveled the lonely highway to DC, he thought about how easily he was able to disregard his consciousness and slip back into a soul that had none- a soul that didn't care for thought or consequences, a soul that willingly destroyed two more black lives, adding to the grim statistics for young Black men, death by homicide.

But now, after the deed was done, his consciousness returned. The soul that was the exact opposite of the one just mentioned began to reassert itself, the soul that understood all the dynamics of a society that produced a sense of self-hate that was so strong it caused Black Men to destroy themselves at a genocidal rate, struggled to possess him. Now that he had time to think, he was filled with a profound sense of guilt. He felt the contradiction that he had become, wanting on the one hand for his people to rise above the self-destructive behavior that plagued his community, but, on the other hand, being a willing instrument of that same self-destructive behavior. At that moment he began to think about a conversation he had with Kenyatta a few months ago on the job. Kenyatta's deep baritone voice and words of wisdom echoed in his ear causing him to feel even more disgusted with himself.

"You know what, youngblood, you going through what a lot of people go through once they become conscious. I went through the same thing. It's very difficult to let go of something you've been holding on to for the better part of your life. This is why it seems as if you're a walking contradiction. Fear not, young brother. The more you study, the more you'll reach the point where you'll be a conscious man with one soul who's not living a life of contradictions. If you keep striving for it, you'll reach it, trust me."

When Kenyatta spoke these words Rafique felt optimistic. At that moment, it had seemed as if his life would take a different path, a path that would lead away from self-destructive behavior. But now, was it too late for him? He certainly felt the pressure of that self-destructive soul asserting its control.

He gripped the steering wheel tightly as the frustration and disappointment in himself began to mount. *Damn, man, I know better. All the shit I learned from that dream and I paid it no mind, as if none of that shit can happen for real. Fuck all that. Them niggas got what they was asking for. That nigga shot my man, and Fuzz slimy ass set him up. As a matter of fact, the nigga asked me that night on the strip did I want to go, knowing they was gonna rob Sean. What if I would've gone? Yeah, but if I wasn't hanging out on the strip, I wouldn't have been there for him to ask me.*

As this thought fled his mind, a scene from his dream immediately filled the void. Rafique could see the four walls of a prison cell and the drab gray paint that covered the walls. He paced the cell, his mind in turmoil as the same internal tug of war was being fought. Moose had just been stabbed and blood was on his hands. The feelings of guilt, justification, disappointment, paranoia, and fear he felt in this dream were the same feelings he felt now.

A car horn blared loudly. Rafique snapped back to reality. He had swerved out of his lane. He quickly swerved back as sweat glossed his forehead. He exhaled loudly as he removed one of his hands from the steering wheel, turned the radio up and filled the car with the soulful sounds of The Whispers.

He needed to drown out the internal conflict of his two warring souls, so he let the romantic sounds of the Whispers take his mind off of those thoughts and allowed Monique's beautiful face to fill his mind. His heart rate quickened in anticipation. He had about an hour's drive left before he reached her home. He stepped on the gas and increased his speed. He needed a release from all the stress he was experiencing, and Monique would be the perfect antidote.

☆ ☆ ☆

One hour and fifteen minutes later Rafique was pulling up on Division Avenue in Northeast Washington DC, where Monique resided. He slowed down in search of a parking space. After circling the block, he finally found one all the way around the corner. After parking and making sure his doors were locked, he jogged quickly back to Division Avenue. It was cold and he needed to get indoors.

He slowed down once he got to approximately where he remembered where her house was, and began squinting to see the addresses. *There it go right there.* Quickly he walked up the steps to her front porch and rang the bell. A couple of minutes passed and no one answered. Just as he was ready to ring the bell again, a soft voice rang out from behind the closed door.

"Who is it?"

"It's Rafique."

He heard the tumblers to the lock give right before the door swung open.

"Oh shit, it's cold out there. Hurry up, Rafique. Shut the door and lock it behind you." Monique said as she hurriedly retreated from the front door.

Rafique locked the door behind him, stepped out of the vestibule and entered her home. Music played softly in the background, as a very slight sweet-smelling fragrance drifted lazily up his nose.

SO YOU'RE HAVING MY BABY,
AND IT MEANS SO MUCH TO MEEEE...
THERE'S NOTHING MORE PRECIOUS,
THAN TO RAISE A FAMILYYY...

Damn this my song, he thought as Jodeci's "Forever My Lady" flowed from the speakers. Rafique sang along with the song and stared at Monique who had taken a seat on the couch. "What's up, Monique, you ain't gonna give me no hug?" he asked after he stopped singing.

Monique smiled, stood up and wrapped her arms around his waist, pressed her body against his, and squeezed tight.

"That's what I'm talking about, you still miss me?" He whispered in her ear.

"Yeah, I miss you," she whispered back.

Reluctantly he let her go and removed his coat and gloves. "Let me get that for you," she said taking his coat and gloves out of his hands and walking seductively towards the closet.

He watched her as her hips swayed hypnotically. *Damn, she look good.* Tearing his eyes away, he took a seat on the couch.

"How was your trip?" she asked, coming back from the closet.

"It was cool, you know, ain't no real traffic on a Monday night."

"Rafique."

"Huh?"

"I'm going upstairs, you coming?" She asked, smiling and biting her bottom lip as she got up. She didn't wait on his response as she headed up the steps.

Rafique was a little surprised by her aggressiveness but that didn't stop him from getting up and following her.

"Rafique, baby, could you turn off the radio and hit that light switch at the bottom of the steps please?" she called out from the top of the stairs.

He stopped before he hit the stairs, turned back, walked over to the stereo system and turned it off. He then headed for the steps and flicked off the light switch, flooding the downstairs in darkness. He then proceeded up the stairs. When he reached the second floor, the sweet-smelling fragrance that he had gotten a whiff of when he first entered the house grew stronger. He inhaled deeply, savoring the smells as he looked down the dimly-lit hallway. Monique was nowhere in sight, but he could see flickering light emanating from a room at the end of the hallway. Rafique smiled and headed that way.

Halfway down the hall, a slow groove erupted from inside the room as Keith Sweat crooned over a pounding drumbeat. Bopping his head in time with the beat, he walked into the entranceway. He stopped, rooted to the spot. The sight that lay before him was as if it came right out of a wet dream. Lit candles were everywhere, filling the room with the sweet smells of jasmine. Red satin sheets and throw pillows covered a king sized bed with a very large mirror for a head board. With her shorts and long tee-shirt discarded on the floor, Monique lay on her side. Her red lace panties clung to her, in stark contrast to her ebony skin tone. Her body, glistening with baby oil, sparkled like a black diamond. But her smile, like the sun after a rainy day, erased away all the stress he had been feeling. Still standing stuck in the doorway, he continued to stare, imprinting on his mind every detail of the sight before him.

"Damn, Rafique, how long you gonna stand there staring?"

"Oh damn, my fault, baby. But you look so fucking good laying there like that."

"Well, I feel even better."

Shaking his head, smiling and coming out his clothes, he approached the bed never taking his eyes off her. He stopped at the foot of the bed, "Come here."

On hands and knees, she crawled across the bed, coming to where he stood. Her eyes moved up his naked body, pausing at his groin and staring lustfully at the aroused state he was in. Moving on past the lean muscles that rippled up his abdomen, her heart throbbed in anticipation as her eyes came to rest at his dark browns.

He smiled, knowing she liked what she saw, as he stared at the reflection of her round ass in the headboard mirror.

"Stand up," he instructed her.

Never leaving the bed, she rose shakily to her feet. She towered above him as she licked her lips. She was ready. Butterflies flew wildly in the pit of his gut and his heart rate kept pace as he reached out and began rubbing her smooth thighs. She gasped at the warmth and strength of his hands as they gently roamed up and down her lower body before coming to rest on her ample backside. He pulled her closed, causing her to stumble a bit, but his strong hands steadied her. Softly, he began kissing her stomach, his lips and tongue dancing, twirling around her naval.

"Uuuuuummmmm," she moaned as her hands slowly raked through his short curly hair.

As he continued to lick and suck, his hands, as if they had a mind of their own, began removing her panties. Taking her hands from his head, she placed them on his shoulders for balance. She lifted one leg and then the other, assisting him in getting her panties off.

"Lay on your back, baby," he said running his finger over her soft spot and causing her to shiver.

She lay on her back obediently, opening her legs wide, invitingly, enticing him to follow. Climbing on the bed, he renewed his kissing. The bitter taste of perfume mixed with salt stained his tongue, but he ignored it. Her soft moans ringing in his ear had him focused on one thing, to please her as well as himself. He could feel the heat emanating from her skin and her warm breath blowing loudly in his ear. Slowly, he moved from her neck to her mouth allowing their tongues to become entwined in an exotic dance. His hands, once again roaming, slipped underneath her bra and began to massage her breasts. Her nipples became erect as they responded to the delicate touch of his fingers as he gently pulled and then released them. He then rubbed his open palm lightly over them causing her once again to moan with pleasure.

"Suck on them, baby, put em in your mouth," she gasped.

Rafique didn't have to be asked twice. He moved from her mouth and began kissing her breast. Slowly he flicked his tongue around the nipple before his lips trapped it in a warm, wet, soft vice and began to suck hard on her sensitive breast, sending sparks throughout her entire body. Frantically, she reached for his manhood and began to pump it furiously.

"Rafique, baby, I want to feel you in me," she cooed pleadingly in his ear.

Without hesitation he gave in to her demands. Arching his back, he raised his ass in the air, grabbed his dick and guided it to her soft spot. Working his hips in a slow circular motion, he entered her. "Sssss uuuummmm," he whispered as her warm wetness engulfed him.

"Does it feel good?" She asked in between breaths as they developed a steady motion.

"Yeah, it feels good." He responded.

Skin slapping against skin could be heard just above the music that continued to play in the background as they made love. With their bodies braided together in a lovers' knot, all the stress and frustration that he had been feeling slowly left his body like the sweat that streamed from his pores. At that moment the only thing that mattered to him was Monique, her shouts of pleasure erasing everything else from his mind.

Hours later, the two lovers lay snuggled up in each other's arms. Wide awake, both of them entertained their own thoughts as the music filled the room. Monique kissed him lightly on the chest before breaking the silence. "Rafique, can I ask you something?"

"Yeah, you can ask me whatever you want."

"Do you remember when we first met and you told me that you was in my first grade class and that you had a crush on me?"

"Yeah." Rafique responded as his heart began to pound in his chest. Somehow he had a feeling where this conversation was going.

"That was game. You wasn't in my first grade class. Who told you my name?"

Just like he thought, he knew that it would come back to this. He didn't answer her right away as he pondered whether or not to tell her the truth.

"Monique, move your head so I can sit up."

Monique lifted her head and Rafique sat up. "I need for you to look at me Mo."

She moved her body and lay across his lap so that she could look up into his eyes.

"What I'm about to tell you gonna sound crazy, but I really need for you to believe me." *She gonna think I'm crazy, she ain't gonna believe this shit.* "Mo, the first time I laid eyes on you was in a dream that I had. That's where I first met you."

"In a dream? Rafique, is you serious?"

"I'm dead serious, Monique. I was in a coma for a week and a day. I had a very bad car accident. When I was in that coma I had this dream that was so real, I still be having trouble believing it was only a dream. I met you in that dream. You see, I was in prison with a life sentence and you were a prison guard. That's how I knew your name. In this dream, we had become real close. I mean we even planned a life together after I got out. I know this sounds crazy Monique, but it's true. When I saw you at work I couldn't believe my eyes. I thought I was going crazy. You see, that's another thing about this dream. You know how it is normally when you dream about something- after awhile you forget about it. But not this dream. Everything in it I remember vividly, like memories. That's why I was staring at you like I was. And then when I asked you was your name Monique and you said 'How did you know my name?' I really thought I had lost it. But I kept my composure. I had to, Mo. I mean, what are the odds that you get to meet the woman of your dreams? Monique, on some real shit, I feel like I was destined to be with you. This is why I'm telling you this- cause I know that what we got right now was meant to be. Mo, I know this shit sound crazy and if the shoe was on the other foot, I would think that you was out of your fucking mind. So I know what I'm asking is a lot, but, Monique, I swear on everything I love, what I just told you is the truth."

She was silent as she contemplated what he had just said. He was absolutely right, she did find what he had told her hard to believe. But the look in his eyes told her that he was telling the truth. She held his gaze for a moment before she responded.

"Rafique, I believe you. You're right, it is hard to believe, but I can see the truth in your eyes. Baby, let me let you in on a little secret. When I first laid eyes on you, physically you were everything that I ever wanted in a man. And then when I got to know you, you were everything that I wanted in a man period. So in a sense, just like you met the woman of your dreams, I met the man of mine. Baby, although I've only known you for a short period of time, I'm loving you like I've loved no other." As she spoke these words, Monique moved up closer and closer to his face until she got close enough to kiss him with all the passion and love she could.

For the next few hours, the new lovers talked. Rafique told Monique all about his dream. Rafique filled her in on all the details, telling her how some of the things he dreamt about had come to pass in real life and how he had changed some other things. He told her about Kenyatta and how similar their circumstances were. Monique lis- tened, fascinated at the things he revealed to her. So much so that she would have stayed up all night listening to his stories, if he would have continued to tell them. But after a while, Rafique kissed her again and ended the storytelling for the night. A little disappointed, she pouted her thick full lips, wanting to hear more.

Rafique ran his fingers through her messed up ponytail. He yawned, "Tomorrow I promise I'll finish telling you, but I'm tired as shit right now, Mo. You drained me, girl. I got to get some rest."

"Alright, Rafique, but tomorrow I got to make you some spinach or some shit, cause you need some more energy." They both laughed as he kissed her on her forehead and held her tight in his arms. Closing his eyes, he had only pleasant thoughts and before long they were both fast asleep.

CHAPTER NINETEEN

A ray of sunlight streaking through a crack in the drawn
curtains beamed directly in Rafique's face. The light
penetrated through his closed eyelids, turning a world of
blackness a shade of blood red. His eyes fluttered slowly for
a brief second before he opened them to slits. As the fog of
sleep dissipated, he shielded his eyes with his hands from
the angry peek of the sun, smacked his mouth a couple
of times, and slowly sat up in the bed. He stretched and
looked around confused at his strange surroundings, and
then she moved in her sleep. It all came back to him, he
was at Monique's.

He smiled thinking about the previous night and how
much better he felt after she bestowed her loving affection
upon him. Glancing to his left, he looked at the digital
alarm clock on her nightstand. It read 11:30 a.m. Carefully, he swung his legs over the side of the bed. He didn't
want to wake her. He needed to get some advice from
his father and he thought it best to go see him alone. If
Monique was with him, he wouldn't be able to discuss the
things he needed to, and if he awakened her, he would be
hard pressed to leave her behind. Very gently, he peeled

the covers from around his lower body and eased out of the bed. Naked, he walked as softly as he could, picked up his clothes off the floor and headed out the bedroom. He paused in mid-stride upon reaching the doorway, hearing her move again. Slowly, he turned around and looked. She was still fast asleep. The covers had shifted as a result of her moving, exposing half her naked body. His manhood stirred, filling up with blood and tempting him to go back, but he resisted the urge. He stared for a moment longer, though, and thanked God for the blessings of allowing this beautiful woman to be a part of his life. At that moment he was being thankful, his mind traveled back to Philly and the woman he left behind. Here he was again, torn between two women. Tracey was his heart, his rock, his best friend, his conscious. When things weren't so good, she was right there standing strong, supporting him with no pressure, and he loved her for that. But his thing with Monique was like an edict from God. It was as if she was created just for him. Although it was all new, it seemed as if she had always been a part of his life. She was the woman of his dreams, a living and breathing fantasy come to life. How could he resist that? He couldn't and he wouldn't.

Slowly, he shook his head. *Fuck that, I did it before with Tracey and Aisha, I'ma do it again. I just got to be careful and not fuck up like I did with Aisha.* As his thoughts began to focus on Aisha, the love that he felt for her had transformed into a blinding hate that he had successfully suppressed. But now as he stood staring at his chocolate angel, these very strong feelings he had for Aisha came flooding back to the surface. *I can't believe that bitch. Fucking my so-called homie. Damn, I don't even know why I'm allowing myself to think about that broad when I got this black goddess laying right in front of me.* Tip-toeing back over to the bed, he gently placed a kiss on her cheek, and then tiptoed out of the bedroom. He had to hurry up. He needed to shower and get dressed before he left to go to his father's house.

After managing to get out of the house without waking Monique, Rafique opened her front door and stepped out into old man winter's frigid embrace. Before he had taken that step outside, he had stolen a quick glance out of her front window and was almost fooled by the sunlight and clear blue skies. Knowing that looks could be deceiving, he dressed according to how one should in late January. Flipping his collar up and tucking his chin, he stepped off the porch and jogged around the corner to his parked car.

Minutes later he sat in his car waiting for it to heat up. Cold air blew from out the heating vents causing him to close them. *Damn, it's taking a long time for this motherfucker to heat up.* He glanced at his gold Bulova and frowned. It was almost twelve thirty. Rapidly drumming his fingers on the steering wheel, he cussed softly under his breath. "Shit, it's getting late. I should've called him to let him know I was coming." He became impatient as he opened the heat vents to see if the car had warmed up. It had. Warm air flowed heavily from the vents, immediately knocking off the chill. He opened up his glove compartment, pulled out his N.W.A. tape, put it in the tape deck, turned the volume up, put the car in drive and pulled off with the sounds of N.W.A. blasting from the speakers.

Fifteen minutes later, Rafique was pulling up on 1st Street. Luckily, he was able to find a parking spot five car lengths from his father's apartment. He parked, turned the car off, locked the doors, got out, and headed for his father's home. A bitterly cold wind gust swept through the street, bringing tears to his eyes and causing him to tuck his chin again and pick up his pace. *Damn, it's cold out here.* Tree limbs stripped of their summer finery, swayed back and forth as gust after gust whisked through the block, infiltrating Rafique's thick layered clothing and placing icy kisses upon his skin.

Rafique reached the apartment building and stepped inside just as another gust of wind blew through the block. The wind smashed against the door and violently slammed it shut behind him. Inside the narrow hallway and shielded from the fierce wind, Rafique took the dusty carpeted steps two at a time to the second floor to his father's apartment. Breathing heavily, vapors appeared in front of his face as he knocked and waited for someone to answer.

"Who is it?" His father's voice called out from behind the closed door.

"It's Rafique."

The lock to the door clicked right before it swung open. "As Salaam Alaikum, Rafique. This is a surprise. Since when you start popping into town unannounced?" Jamil said, standing in the doorway, smiling before retreating back inside.

"Wa Laikum Salaam, Abbee. Is Lorraine here?" Rafique asked, stepping inside the house and closing the door behind him.

"Naw, she's around the corner, over her mother's house. Why?"

"I need to talk to you in private, that's why." He responded, removing his coat, hat and gloves. Walking over to the closet, he hung them up, before taking a seat on the couch.

Jamil sat in his favorite chair, pulled out a Marlboro Light and lit it up. "What's up, son? What's going on?"

Rafique hesitated for a moment. With his eyes downcast, he struggled for the words. "Abbee, I messed up, man."

"You messed up? What you talking about? Messed up how?"

"I don't know how to tell you this."

"Why don't you just try and say whatever it is you have to say."

Rafique looked up and gazed into his father's eyes. He saw the look of concern before he quickly dropped his eyes back to the floor. The shame that he felt was overwhelming. How could he justify his actions to his father? He knew no matter how he tried to spin it, the conversation he was about to have was going to end with a severe checking. With his voice barely above a whisper and his eyes still glued to the floor, he began speaking, "Abbee, man, these niggas...,"

"Ho...hold up, what you mean, these niggas? Rafique, ain't you the one that sat right here in that same spot a couple of months ago and questioned me and my commitment to our people? But then you come in here today and you use that word. Out of all the words to use you come in here and the first thing out of your mouth is 'these niggas'."

"Abbee it ain't that deep. It's just, you know, a slang. It ain't the same thing as when a white person uses it. It's just a figure of speech."

"Slang? A figure of speech? Do you know how insane that sounds? What you've just demonstrated is a sickness that's pervasive throughout the black community. I mean, here you are a so-called conscious black man using a term that was specifically coined to degrade and to dehumanize a whole race of people. When they kidnapped our ancestors and packed them on slave ships like sardines, they called them niggers. When they brutalized us for over three hundred years in chattel slavery, they called us niggers. When they were lynching us for over a hundred years, they were calling us niggers. Rafique, thousands upon thousands of black men, women and children- before their lives were brutally extinguished- the last word that they heard was nigger. This is why history is so very important, because when you become disconnected from your past, you forget these things, and as a direct result of that disconnection, you have a lot of black people thinking its okay to call one another nigga. They make excuses by saying it's a term of endearment, or like you just said, a figure of speech, slang, or they say it's just a reflection of ghetto life. Rafique, you can't use these excuses because intellectually they don't stand up. You see, historically nigger meant that we were considered and treated as a people who are stupid and lazy, deserving to be enslaved, castrated, lynched, sold like a pierce of furniture, and murdered. In other words, treated as something less than a human being. Rafique, this is the legacy of the word in which you choose to use in describing your people. I don't care if you hate whoever it is you're calling a nigger, it's still not an acceptable term to use because if one black person is a nigger, then we all are. So I would appreciate it if you still intend to use that term, never use it in my presence again." With his brow creased in an angry scowl, Jamil took a drag from his cigarette, glared at Rafique and waited for him to respond.

Humbled, Rafique slowly lifted his head up and matched his father's stare. "You right, I know better, but that's part of the reason why I had to talk to you. Abbee, I got myself into a serious situation. I mean—you see how I was just like, 'these niggas' — it's like although I know better, I keep falling back into this street shit. It seems like no matter what I know, how differently I see things, or how I try to live my life, I keep allowing myself to be dragged into some self-destructive shit. I mean, Abbee, it's like I don't have the strength to resist the influence of those streets."

"Let me get this straight. You came all the way out here on a weekday out of the clear blue to tell me this? Rafique, you could have called. What the fuck is going on, son?" Knowing his son had something major going on in his life and he was beating around the bush, Jamil's concern grew as he pushed him for answers.

Rafique watched his father pull hard on his cigarette and took his time answering. "Abbee…" He paused, trying to think of the right way to say what he had to say. Then it dawned on him, the only way to say it, was just to say it. "Abbee, I killed somebody."

Having taken a drag off his cigarette as his son spoke these words, violent coughs racked Jamil's body as he choked on the smoke. After a short moment, tears brimmed in his eyes as the last vestiges of his coughing fit subsided. Clearing his throat, he spoke, his tone carefully measured. "What happened, Rafique?"

"Abbee, it don't matter what happened, how it happened, or who it happened to. You know, what's done is done. I just need to know what to do now."

"It don't matter what happened? How the fuck can you come to me for help and then you won't tell me what the fuck is going on? How can I tell you what to do when I don't know the details? Now, I'm going to ask you one more time, what happened?"

Rafique dropped his head again as he unraveled the story. "To make a long story short, a friend of mine got shot so I got the two dudes that shot him." Rafique was very careful not to mention his dream and the effect it had on him regarding his feelings towards Fuzz.

"Rafique, you killed two people? Goddamn, son, did anybody see you?"

"Naw, ain't nobody see me."

"Are you sure?"

"Yeah," he lied. He couldn't be sure if anyone saw him or not.

"Can anyone connect you to these people?"

"Naw."

"What did you do with the gun?"

"I got rid of it. I threw it in the sewer hole in another part of the city."

"Who knows about this?"

"Besides you, nobody."

"Are you sure about that? What about that girl you live with?"

"Look, I'm sure. I ain't tell her nothing."

"I can't believe this shit. That's two more black lives lost with a third hanging in the balance. First thing you need to do is pray and ask Allah for his forgiveness."

As the word forgiveness left his father's mouth, that strange sense of déjà vu engulfed Rafique. For a split second, the image of that dream flooded his consciousness.

The picture in his mind was so vivid it was as if it were a memory from the previous day instead of a several month old dream. With clarity, he could see the clothes his father wore and the troubled expression that marked his face. It was the same expression that marked his father's face now, the deep wrinkles that creased his forehead, and the worry that showed in his eyes. He could hear the music from the car radio just above the sounds of the traffic as Phyllis Hyman's sultry voice rode the waves of heartbreak in song. He could feel the concern that betrayed his father's voice as they cruised through the Washington D.C. streets, just like he could feel it now as he sat in his father's front room. But it wasn't the images that caused this strange sense of déjà vu, it was the words. The words his father spoke then were the same ones he spoke now. Like an echo from the past, the words rang in his ear. "Rafique, you need to pray and ask Allah for his forgiveness." The frustration he felt when he heard the words in his dream he felt at this very moment. Out of all the advice he father could give this was the best he could come up with - pray.

Dazed, his heart pounding, fear began to assert itself within him. *What the fuck? Why does everything in that fucking dream keep happening in real life?*

"Rafique, did you hear what I just said?" Jamil asked, seeing the dazed look in his son's eyes.

"Huh? Uh, yeah, yeah." Rafique responded, shaking off thoughts of his dream and that weird feeling of déjà vu. Frustration immediately returned, filling the void left by the thoughts and feelings he had just shaken off. *Why the fuck he always bringing up praying and religion? I just told him I killed two people and he gonna say I need to pray.* Letting his frustration bubble over, he expressed what he was thinking without any thought as to how his father would respond.

"Abbee, I don't mean any disrespect, but is that the best advice you can give, pray? I just told you I killed two people. I mean, what if some how the police find out? I need some practical advice. Something that can help me right now, not after I die.

"Who the fuck you think you talking to? You came to me, remember? You asking me to help you. Not only that, I'm you father, you don't disrespect me like that."

"You know what, man, I'm sorry. I got to go; I ain't come here for this."

"You ain't come here for this? You really have lost your fucking mind. You just think you can talk to me anyway you think, huh?"

Rafique didn't respond as he got up, walked to the closet and grabbed his coat. Putting his coat on, he looked at his father and said, "Abbee, I love you man, but to avoid me saying something that I know I'll regret, I'ma just leave. I ain't going back to Philly no time soon, so I'll be back after we both calm down so we can talk again."

"Rafique, if you leave out this door right now, don't come back." Jamil said, standing up.

"What, don't come back?" You see, that's why I got to leave man, you treating me like I'm a little fucking kid. Abbee, I'm a grown man."

"So, you think because you're grown, you can't be checked?"

"Yo, man, I'm done with this right now. I'm out."

"Rafique, Rafique!" Jamil called out to his son, but he was ignored as Rafique left out of the apartment and slammed the door shut behind him.

The sound of the door slamming was like a gunshot at an indoor firing range. The vibrations rattled the small apartment as Jamil stood and stared at the door. *Goddamn it, why the fuck did I do that?* Now that he was beginning to calm down, he felt bad about how he reacted. In his time of need, Rafique came to him, asking him for his help and instead of him helping, he got angry and literally chased his son away. *He'll be back,* he thought. Jamil hoped the best for his son as he sat back down in his favorite chair. Absently, he picked up his cigarettes and felt the wrinkled pack. *Damn, I'm almost out.* He took one out anyway, lit it up and took a deep drag. He blew the smoke out as the nicotine calmed his nerves. With his eyes closed, he said a silent prayer asking God to forgive and to protect his son.

As soon as Rafique stepped outside, the wind, as if it were stalking him, came out of nowhere and smacked him in the face. He was so full of anger, though, that the wind's frigid caress was but a minor irritation as he trudged to his car. With his mind replaying over and over the argument he had with his father, he paid no mind to the black Eagle Talon that slowly cruised down the block until he heard a horn beep. Looking up, he recognized the car immediately. It was his brother Pluck, and his cousin Chad. Bypassing his car, he walked in the street and opened the back door to Pluck's brand new ride.

"What's up, Fique?" Pluck said as Rafique got in and shut the door behind him.

Warm air enveloped him, reminding him of how cold it was outside, as he spoke back. "What's up, Pluck? What's up, Chad? Damn, Pluck, I see you ain't have to wait for your graduation before you start playing with your present."

"Yeah, well you know, that's what happens when you graduate at the top of your class. This motherfucker nice, though, ain't it?"

"Yeah, it's nice. Damn, what's up Chad?"

"What's up, Fique?" Chad responded.

"Aw, man, I just got finished arguing with my pop, but other than that I'm cool. What's up with y'all? Where y'all going?"

"We getting ready to go back to the house. I was just stopping around here to see my mom and the kids." Pluck said.

"Your mom ain't here, she's around the corner. She got Ali and Lachele with her. You know what, since you mentioned it, I'ma go see Muhammad and them a little later on."

"Yeah, man, you definitely need to go see him, he always asking for his big brother." Pluck said.

"Ay, Fique, man, what's up wit your shorty fucking around wit Dre?" Chad asked."

"Man fuck her and Dre." Rafique responded.

"Yeah, that nigga Dre a fucking bama Joe. He supposed to be your boy. How he gonna do some foul shit like that?" Pluck chimed in.

"Yo, man, that's just how some niggas carry it. It ain't no thing, though. I got me another girl from out Northeast. A pretty chocolate motherfucker."

"Oh yeah, she got some girlfriends?" Chad asked.

"I don't know. I'ma find out, though. As a matter of fact, I'm out. I left her asleep this morning. She probably mad as shit. I ain't say nothing before I left. I'm about to go back over there."

"How long you gonna be in town?" Pluck asked.

"I'ma be out here for a minute. I ain't going back to Philly for a while."

"What, you gonna be staying wit shorty?" Pluck asked.

"Yeah, I'ma be back here a little later, though. I'ma let my pop cool off some first, though."

"Alright then, Joe, we gonna be in the house. We ain't doing nothing today." Pluck said.

"Alright, Pluck. Alright, Chad. I'ma see y'all later."

"Alright, Fique," they both responded.

Rafique left Pluck and Chad, hurried to his car, got in, closed the door and started it up. As he waited for the car to heat up, he began to think of Aisha and how she betrayed him. *I'm going over there. Yeah, that's what I'ma do. I'ma go over there, act like I want her back, fuck her, make her call that nut ass nigga Andre up and tell him she don't want him no more and then I'ma shit on her. I'ma call Monique right in her face and then I'ma leave.*

As these thoughts played in his mind, he began to think of his dream and how Aisha and Tracey's roles had reversed. In his dream, Tracey was the slimy one, but now it was Aisha. He smiled at this thought. Aisha was going to pay for both times he had been betrayed, even if one of the events wasn't real.

CHAPTER TWENTY

He snored like an old steam engine train all through the night without interruption and Aisha hated it. It had gotten so bad for her that she had to wear earplugs, and even with the plugs, some nights he snored so loud, it rendered them useless.

Aisha stood in the bathroom and gazed at her reflection. She was tired and her face showed it. Her eyes were baggy and blood shot red, and for the last five minutes, she had been scrubbing her face to rid herself of that tired look, but she was unsuccessful. She shook her head, yawned and left out of the bathroom. Last night was one of those nights where sleep was as elusive as the Loch Ness Monster.

Aisha walked past her bedroom. She could hear Andre's loud snoring, she frowned, shook her head, and continued to the living room. If not for that one very irritating fact, the relationship that she had with him would be perfect. He provided her with all the attention and love she had been missing. He put her on a pedestal, treating her like a queen. He could be sensitive and at the same time put his foot down when she got out of hand. The sex was okay, but she was teaching him, and with him being an eager student, on top of the numerous lessons she was giving out, she knew that the sex would pick up. So why wasn't she satisfied? Why did she constantly think about Rafique? Why did she hope it was him calling every time the phone rang? Why did she imagine it was Rafique she wrapped her legs around every time she made love to Andre? She picked up the remote from the coffee table, took a seat on the couch and turned on the television. It was almost time for her favorite soap opera to come on. *I like Andre, but I don't love him. I'm not being fair to him, cause he love the shit out of me and I still got all these unresolved feelings. I jumped into this relationship too fast. I should have waited. Plus, I think the only reason why I gave him some so fast was because I wanted to make Rafique mad. This ain't right what I'm doing, but he treats me so good. I'ma just give it some time. The more time that goes by the less I'll think about Rafique and the more of myself I'll be able to give Andre.*

KNOCK...KNOCK...KNOCK...

Loud knocking on the door snapped her from her thoughts. *Who the fuck is this knocking on my door like that?* Clearly agitated, she got up from the couch and went to answer the door.

✵ ✵ ✵

Rafique made a right at North Capital Street and pulled into the Fort Totten apartment complex parking lot. He had no trouble finding a parking spot. It was still early in the afternoon and most of the residents were at work. He killed the engine, opened the door and stepped out into the brilliant sunshine and extreme cold. Rafique made sure the doors were locked; an unlocked car would be a bonanza for all the crackheads that roamed throughout Fort Totten. He then shut the door and proceeded up the walkway that led to the three five-story apartment buildings that made up the complex.

A light stream of drug addicts bustled back and forth, braving the frigid temperatures to satisfy that insatiable urge to feed their addictions. "Ay, youngin, you doing something?" A crackhead asked from behind him as Rafique continued up the walkway.

He turned to see who it was that was speaking to him and stared in disgust. It was a young man probably the same age as he was, and he was filthy. His light blue jeans with big holes in the knees looked as if he had rolled around under a car. Rafique could see his dirty long johns through the holes and he knew that this guy probably had on these same filthy clothes for months. He had on about three different spring jackets draped over his emaciated body, all of them grimy. To top off his filthy appearance, he adorned a dusty Oakland Raider ski hat. Rafique looked at the man and thanked God that it was cold and windy because he knew the man smelled awful. Rafique shook his head and kept going with the crackhead right behind him.

Coming up on the middle building he could see his homie Ern standing in the doorway. "Yo, Ern!" He shouted out.

Ern turned in the direction he heard his name being called, his face lighting up as he saw Rafique approach. "Yo, what's up, youngin," he said once Rafique reached him. "What's going on? When you get in town?"

Before Rafique could respond, the dusty crackhead interrupted. "You doing something, youngin?" He asked Ern.

"Motherfucker, don't you see me talking! Wait over there by the fence until I'm done. Fuck is wrong with you?"

Humbled, the crackhead shuffled away to wait. Used to the very bad treatment that crackheads received, Rafique paid no mind to Ern's outburst. He smiled, removed his glove and stuck out his hand. "What's up, Ern? I just got in last night."

Ern removed his glove, firmly shook Rafique's hand and then pulled him close, briefly embracing him. "Yeah, man, I'm out here on my grind. I got to get this money. You see me out here carrying it like a fucking mailman. You know the saying – through rain, sleet or snow. I'ma true hustler. You see, I'm the only nigga out here. The rest of the so-called hustlers out here still in the fucking bed. They satisfied with the measly couple of dollars they getting. Fique, man, I ain't trying to do this shit for the rest of my life. Ain't no retirement plans in this game. So I'ma hustle hard, stack as much paper as I can, get out the game and parlay this paper into something legitimate."

Rafique nodded his head and continued to smile. Ern liked to talk and he knew that if he said one word, Ern would go on for hours. It was definitely too cold for that, so he cut the conversation short. "Ay, Ern, let me run in here for a minute. I need to holla at Aisha."

"Alright, man. Ay, you know she been seeing your boy. That big, black, bama ass nigga from around on First Street."

"Yeah, I know."

"Alright then, youngin, I'ma be out here when you finish."

"Alright, Ern."

Rafique walked pass Ern, entered the apartment building and headed up the stairs to Aisha's apartment.

✲ ✲ ✲

Without even saying who is it, Aisha snatched open her door with a torrid of cuss words ready to roll off her tongue.

The words evaporated before they could escape her vocal chords, turning into nothingness as she stared at Rafique standing in her front door. Her heart roared, pounding, the vibrations rattling her entire body. She covered her mouth with her hand and gasped.

"What's up ,Eesh? Surprised?" He said with a sly smirk on his face.

All the feelings she had been trying to stifle came pouring to the surface. But like a master of disguise, she hid the love behind a mask of anger. She regained her composure and sucked her teeth before responding. "Rafique, what you want?"

"I want you."

"You want me? It's too late to be wanting me now. When you had me you should've just held on."

"I should've held on? How could I when you crossed me like you did?"

"Rafique, you lost me before that incident with Andre."

"Look, man, why is we standing in the hallway? Is you gonna let me in or what?"

"No, Rafique, you can't come in." Although she said she didn't want to let him, she really did, but she couldn't with Andre asleep in her bedroom. If she could just get him to go home, she could get rid of Andre and then call him back over. These were her thoughts, but Rafique wasn't a mind reader.

"What you mean, I can't come in? Move the fuck out the way."

"No, Rafique, this is my house and I don't want you in here. Furthermore, we ain't like that no more anyway. You can't just come in my house whenever you feel like it. What if I got company in here?"

Hearing these words sparked a rage so intense that he lost all self-control. "Bitch, get the fuck out the way!" He shoved her hard, sending her flying back in the house and crashing to the floor.

"Pussy! Don't be putting your hands on me!"

He had let his emotions get the better of him and he immediately felt bad about shoving her so hard. He stepped into her apartment and bent down to help her up. With his focus on Aisha, he was unaware of Andre who now stood in the living room, gun in hand. Aisha crashing to the floor and shouts of rage had awakened him.

"Rafique? You bitch ass nigga! You like putting your hands on girls, huh? Well, you put your hands on the wrong one this time."

The only thing Rafique had time to do was look up as the loud retort of Andre's nine millimeter exploded inside the small apartment. A piercing scream originating from deep within Aisha's soul was the next thing he heard – right before what felt like a mule kick and a searing burning hot pain exploded in his chest. Then, everything went black.

CHAPTER TWENTY-ONE

BEEP-BEEP-BEEP-BEEP-BEEP

The unremitting beep of the heart monitor was the only sound in the room. After hours of surgery, whether he lived or died would depend upon how his body responded to the trauma that had been inflicted upon it. The doctors did all they could do. Now it was up to him.

BBBBBBEEEEEEPPPPPP

Flat line, the trauma was too much.

Hearing the alarm triggered by the flat line on the heart monitor, one doctor and one nurse rushed into the room. Immediately the doctor checked for a pulse. There was none. He shook his head and pulled the sheet over the body. Looking at the nurse, holding an ink pen and clipboard in her hands, he cleared his throat and with all the emotion of a robot he spoke. "Rafique Johnson…Cause of death," as the doctor dictated the nurse jotted down what he said. "Cause of death, multiple stab wounds to the upper torso. Nurse, you can call Graterford and let them know they can pick up the body."

"Yes, doctor, right away," the nurse responded right before they left out of the intensive care unit, leaving Rafique's lifeless body lying on the table.

THE END...

Excerpts from the next novel
by Terrel Carter: <u>Tainted Souls</u>

TAINTED SOULS
By Terrel Carter

Philadelphia, PA
1971

Like a scared child clinging to his mother, his soul fought to keep its grip on life as the oxygen-rich blood flowing through his veins slowly drained away. Obenga knew the minute he decided to take a stand and fight against the centuries of oppression and racism that black people throughout this land had endured he would most likely end up this way. History was littered with examples of black men and women who were assassinated once they chose the path of resistance, and just like those who came before him, the hot metal that ripped through his flesh would add one more to the list of fallen heroes.

Lying on his back, his eyes scanned the dark heavens as tears left trails of salt down the sides of his ebony cheeks. He had let his guard down on this night due to the overwhelming sense of joy that he felt for the birth of his twins. Just like a boxer who lets his guard down and pays for it by getting hit with a crushing left hook and loss of consciousness,

Obenga was paying with his life, after getting hit with something far more devastating than a hook.

Earlier that day he had been at one of the safe houses the Black Liberation Army had scattered throughout the city. Working late as he always did, he was interrupted by the phone ringing. Picking it up on the third ring, he spoke into the receiver, "Hello."

"Obenga! This Carol from next door. Rachel just went into labor. She on her way to the hospital right now!"

"Alright, Carol, thank you, I'm on my way." Hanging up the phone, Obenga was elated. At twenty-five this would be his first experience with childbirth. His heart raced with anticipation as he stood up and looked around the cluttered apartment. He then gathered up the guerilla warfare texts he had been working on, turned out the lights, locked up the apartment, and left the building.

The loud roar of a bad muffler filled the night as Obenga sped down the street in his beat up Volkswagen, on his way to Philadelphia General Hospital. With the street lights whizzing by in his peripheral vision, he began to think of his organization and the new direction it was heading in. The Black Liberation Army (BLA) was an offshoot of the Black Panther Party and was brought into existence out of necessity. After the Party was brought to its knees by governmental infiltration, assassinations, and imprisonment the remaining members decided that a new autonomous strike force to handle all defensive armed actions was needed. New to the organization and full of youthful exuberance, Obenga joined immediately. Soon after its inception, the BLA launched planned counterstrikes on police stations throughout the city. Taking a page from Mao Tao Tsung, they employed hit-and-run guerilla warfare tactics. Whenever one of their members or anybody from the community was murdered or assaulted by the police, the BLA moved into action. These planned counterstrikes were carried out so swiftly and efficiently that the only dead and wounded left behind were the police.

Although the BLA still suffered casualties, now there was accountability. Gone were the days when Police Commissioner Rizzo could have the Party's headquarters raided and its members paraded naked in the streets at gunpoint. The days of the Gestapo-like police tactics had come to an end. There would be no more assassinations and false imprisonments without retribution. The pendulum was beginning to show some balance. The time for change had finally arrived.

After only a short period of time Obenga became a known member of the BLA. He knew as a result he was a direct target of the police, but his overwhelming sense of joy on this night dulled the paranoia that normally kept him on point.

He could see the flashing lights of the police car in his rearview mirror two blocks away from the hospital. Pulling over, he put the car in park and reached under his seat for the Snub Nose .38 that he kept with him. 'Damn it! I left my piece back at the apartment.' A strong sense of apprehension overtook his senses but he shook it off thinking to himself everything would be okay, his babies were about to be born. God couldn't be so cruel as to let something happen to him now. What he forgot to take into account was the fact that God works in mysterious ways and sometimes his ways work contrary to how we would like them to.

"Could you please step out of the vehicle," Officer Ian Fitzpatrick directed Obenga, as he and his partner slowly approached with their weapons drawn.

✫ ✫ ✫

The time in between contractions became shorter and the pain more intense as Rachel moved closer to giving birth. She felt alone in a crowded room full of nurses and doctors as she searched in vain for her man. 'Where is he?' she thought as another contraction ripped through her swollen womb.

Checking to see if her cervix had dilated enough, the doctor looked up from between her legs and said, "Rachel, it's time, take a deep breath and push."

✲ ✲ ✲

"You one of them Black Panther Niggers, ain't ya?" Officer Fitzpatrick asked as he cautiously approached Obenga.

Stifling his rage, Obenga raked his hands across the hood of his car lodging paint chips under his fingernails. Keeping his hands glued to the hood, he twisted his head around and addressed the police, "Look man, my wife is in the hospital right now having a baby. I ain't done nothing wrong. I'm just trying to get to the hospital."

"You ain't done nothing wrong? Tell that to the guys you fuckers murdered in cold blood from the eighteenth district. Those were some real good friends of mine!"

"Look man, I'm sorry about your friends, but I ain't have nothing to do with it." As his heart pounded in his chest, Obenga knew that he was in a perilous situation. With his mind in overdrive he frantically tried to think of way out of the dire straits he found himself in.

"I don't think you gonna make it to see that baby nigger of yours come into the world. I think a few days down at the district will do you a bit of good. What you think, McCall?" Fitzpatrick asked his nervous rookie partner.

Eyes wide as a crack fiend inhaling a blast of cocaine, and his hands shaking like leaves, McCall shouted out, "The

Nigger's got a gun!" Without hesitation he then opened fire. Fitzpatrick followed suit, emptying his revolver into a defenseless Obenga.

The force from the bullets tearing through his slim frame spun him around before he fell on his back, the back of his head slamming against the cold hard concrete. Losing consciousness for a moment, Obenga could see with his mind's eye his lovely wife as she went through the agony of childbirth all on her own.

"This your first nigger?" Fitzpatrick asked his partner who stood staring in shock. "Aw, don't worry about it, he had it coming. These animals murdered some real good officers. You got the throwaway partner?" Fitzpatrick asked as calmly as if he had just stepped on a bug.

McCall's voice shook a little as he responded, "Yea, hold up a minute." Bending over, he retrieved a .22 from an ankle holster.

"Go on; put it in his hand so we can call this thing in." Fitzpatrick instructed him.

Regaining consciousness, Obenga's eyes fluttered open. He was helpless as the police planted a gun in his hand. With each second that ticked by his breathing became more and more labored until, finally, he took one more breath and breathed no more.

At that very same instant, Rachel gave one last push and her second son came out of her womb, joining his brother in a world that would be just as dark for them as the one they had just left behind...

A MESSAGE FROM THE AUTHOR...

At the age of twenty-three I would have never imagined that for the next eighteen years of my life I would be residing, in a state correctional facility. I hadn't seriously learned how to weigh the consequences of my actions, and whether the risks were worth the superficial rewards.

As a result of my ignorance I was out there moving faster than the speed of thought, unconsciously caught in an intricate web of self-destruction. As I slept walked through life, greedily chasing material gains, I made the mistake that many young brothers make; I took my life and freedom for granted. I valued things that weren't important. Those things that would ultimately put my life into the hands of others who judged me, not knowing me. Thus, ensuring that I would lose one of my most precious possessions. My freedom.

Now eighteen years later as I sit behind a forty foot, razor wire, steel rod reinforced, concrete wall, I look back on my life and sadly shake my head, because now I understand. I now realize that the things that I once valued was nothing more than a fool's treasure, gained at the expense of other people's misery. I did the math and it just didn't add up right. Nothing I possessed or could have obtained, ripping and running through the unforgiving streets equaled my life.

I sacrificed myself for nothing. Time waits for no one, so as I close in on my second decade behind these walls, those that came before me continue to populate penitentiary graveyards, never getting the chance to walk as free men again. Life in the state of Pennsylvania means just that, you get out only in a box. Like I said in the beginning of this missive, I never thought that this could happen to me. So, to all my young brothers who can read these words, don't think like I used to. Cause when I look around at the faces of those trapped in the bowels of the belly of the beast, what I couldn't imagine at the age of 23 is what I see now. The faces that stare back at me are just like me. They are just like you...

ORDER FORM

iDream Publications
P.O. Box 28910
Philadelphia, PA 19151

Name: _____

SBI #: _____ (if applicable)

Address: _____

City/State: _____

Zip Code: _____

Quantity: _____

Cost: $15.00 + shipping & handling of $4.95
Add $1.00 to postage for each additional purchase
Shipping & handling to prisons…..FREE

Please make money orders and
institutional checks payable to:
iDream Publications

Allow five to seven business days for delivery.

Thank You.